The Young and the Restless

10
SHINING STAR

William J. Bell and Lee Phillip Bell, Co-Creators,
Executive Producers, and Head Writers

Soaps™ & Serials

PIONEER COMMUNICATIONS NETWORK, INC.

Shining Star

THE YOUNG AND THE RESTLESS paperback novels are published and distributed by Pioneer Communications Network, Inc.

SOAPS & SERIALS™ is a trademark of Pioneer Communications Network, Inc.

ISBN: 0-916217-80-9

Printed in Canada

10 9 8 7 6 5 4 3 2 1

SHINING STAR

Chapter One

Shattered Dreams

Wearily, Stuart Brooks turned from the window. His hands were shaking, but he was too tired to care. With one stupid mistake he'd flushed his very life down the sewer. After the past few years of loneliness, he'd been just about to grab at happiness again, only to find a wall thrown up in his way at the last minute. He felt much older than his years, more like the grandfather of four grown daughters than their father. Too old, certainly, to have been caught by such stupidity. He righted his chair, then sat down.

"I'd like my doctor to check into your . . . allegation," Stuart said.

Jill Foster sat across from him, her young body a ripe and ready temptation for any man. She batted her eyes at him and tossed her long red hair over one shoulder. "Is your doctor a gynecologist?"

The heat of anger filled his face. Was she laughing at him? Was this cheap woman playing with him?

"Would you believe it if my doctor tells you I'm pregnant?" she asked, placing a letter on his desk.

Stuart reached for the letter. There were other things on his desk—letters from subscribers protesting his editorial policy, notes on breaking stories and investigations, even notice of an award his newspaper had won for an unprecedented fourth time—but none of them held any interest for him as he unfolded the letter Jill had brought him.

The stationery was that of Dr. Michael Jamison. Stuart didn't know the doctor personally, but recognized him as a well-known and highly reputable gynecologist in Genoa City. The letter was routine in nature, addressed to Jill and advising her, since she was expecting, to give up cigarettes and alcohol, get her rest, and eat properly.

The anger drained from Stuart's body as the horrible realization that Jill was telling the truth chilled him. He was the father of her child.

A flicker of hope sputtered suddenly within him. No, she hadn't proven that. All she had proven was that she was pregnant. Who knew who the father was?

Knowing Jill, it could be any male in
Genoa City between the ages of fourteen
and eighty-five. He handed the letter back
to her.

"The doctor's telephone number is on
this letter," she said with a smile, holding
the paper up. "If you'd like to call him."

Stuart took a deep breath, gripping the
arms of his chair. His hands were no
longer shaking, though anger still coursed
through his veins. "What would be the
purpose of that? All Dr. Jamison could do
is tell me you're pregnant. Does he have
some magic way of knowing if I am indeed the child's father?"

Jill carefully and deliberately folded the
letter and returned it to her purse before
she looked back up at Stuart. When she
did, her eyes were dark with rage. "As I
understand it," she said, her voice sur-
prisingly calm and controlled, "the only
test that will indicate paternity is a blood
test after the baby is born. And even then,
it's not positive proof." She smiled slightly. "I guess you'll just have to take my
word for it."

Stuart had to turn away from the cool,
calculating look in her eyes or he would
have thrown something at her. Damn her.
Damn himself for falling prey to her long
legs and full lips.

"Do you want your child born a bastard?" Jill continued, speaking to his back. "And do you want all the publicity that will result? If I have to go to court to force you to submit to a blood test, there's no way this town will ignore it."

"It can be done privately," Stuart pointed out.

"I don't think so." Jill's smile grew, though there wasn't a flicker of humor in her eyes. "There are so many things that would have to be ironed out. Child support. The child's name."

Stuart stared out the office window toward a park on the west side of town. Though he couldn't actually see her house from here, he knew that Liz lived across from the park, and he'd gotten in the habit of looking that way whenever he was troubled. Looking that way, and finding peace in the thought of the woman he loved. Except that today it didn't work. The knowledge that he had betrayed Liz's love—betrayed her love with her *daughter* —weighed heavily on his heart.

Oh, God. How had he been so stupid to succumb to that harlot? He should have run from the room when he'd seen her. Las Vegas had been full of professionals. He should have hired one if his desires had to be satisfied. Then his and Liz's lives would still be intact.

A shudder went through his whole

body. Liz was such a wonderful, decent woman. What had she done to deserve this? If only he could take all the suffering and save her the pain. None of this was her fault; she didn't deserve to be hurt.

"What do you want me to do, Stuart?" Jill's voice was soft and quiet, but Stuart wasn't fooled. He wished then that he could lose himself like Leslie. Stuart almost broke down and cried as the picture of his beautiful, sensitive daughter floated into his mind. His first wife dead, Leslie gone, and now he was going to lose another woman he loved. What had he done to deserve this black cloud?

He took a deep breath, knowing he couldn't run. He never had before. Besides, where could he hide? Where could he hide from his guilt and his self-loathing? There was no need to ask what he'd done to deserve this black cloud; he had brought it on himself. His own weakness in the face of temptation was what had caused it. He had sinned and had to pay the price. The possibility was there that the child was his; he could not turn his back on his own flesh and blood. He turned slowly around to face her.

"I'll marry you." His voice echoed hollowly in his ears, a mockery of the flowing words of love he'd used when he proposed to Liz just a few weeks back.

"How nice. I'd love to be Mrs. Stuart Brooks," Jill said.

The smile spreading across her face was like the morning sun bathing a meadow, but he would not be taken in by her beauty again. "In name only," he added.

Jill's face wrinkled in a silent question.

"I will marry you," Stuart said. "I will support you and the child, but I will never share your bed."

She shrugged, either not believing him or not caring. "Whatever you say, Stuart, but I'll love, honor, and obey you the rest of my natural life."

It should have been Liz saying this to him, not Jill. He turned back to the window, to the sight of that little park outside of town, but met up with guilt and remorse. What had he done?

"Now comes the hard part, Patsy," the older woman said.

The young ex–cocktail waitress lifted her shining face from the bundle she carried in her arms. Her eyes were bright and contented. "What hard part, Margot?" Patsy asked.

"Losing that extra twenty pounds you put on for the baby," Margot replied. The bartender and the few patrons sitting nearby laughed.

"Bart likes me this way," Patsy said, her

soft, milk-fed cheeks glowing with the joy of being pleasing to her man.

Leslie had just been standing with them at the back of the nightclub, staring at the baby. The conversation whirled around her as the sight of the innocent child tugged at her heart. "Can I hold her?" she asked suddenly.

Patsy turned to look at her. "Oh, Patsy," Margot said. "I don't think Leslie was working here when you left, was she? She plays the piano and sings. And boy, are tips good when she's on."

Patsy's blue eyes were soft as she smiled. "Sure, Leslie. You can hold her."

"Just don't sing to her," Margot added with a chuckle. "Or Patsy'll never get her to go to sleep for her."

Leslie's arms reached for the baby, automatically fitting securely around the little body. The baby blinked momentarily, but soon settled against Leslie's breasts with a gurgle of contentment.

Leslie's body and spirit suddenly were at peace, as if the past weeks of confusion and uncertainty had never happened. She still had no idea who she was beyond the fact that her first name was Leslie, no idea where she had come from or why. But standing here with the little baby in her arms, she felt whole and alive again. She felt as if she and the baby were one.

"How many kids do you have?" Patsy asked.

The words dragged Leslie back from her rose garden into the dim red lights and stale cigarette smoke of the nightclub. Leslie stared at the woman.

"I was wondering how many kids you had," the baby's mother repeated.

Confusion marred the contentment within Leslie. Confusion and fear as she faced once more the black wall that separated her from her past. Her muscles tightened and the baby stirred uneasily. "I don't know," she mumbled.

"I beg your pardon?"

Patsy's soft blue eyes were clouded; the baby was starting to fuss.

"I don't have any children," Leslie said.

But Patsy was more interested in her baby than in Leslie's answer. "Here, let me take her," she said. "She may need changing."

She took the baby back, leaving Leslie feeling alone and lost again. Jonas, the owner of the nightclub, came up behind Leslie and put his hand on her shoulder. It should have felt comforting; it should have eased her fears and loneliness; but it did nothing.

"Use my office to change her if you want," Jonas told Patsy.

Patsy nodded, hurrying away. With the baby gone from sight, Leslie felt the emptiness overwhelm her. She moved about the recesses of her mind, amid the doors locked on her past. So many barriers, but memories seemed to be trying to get out. There was scratching behind those locked doors.

"She's as happy as a pig in slop."

Leslie forced herself to look at Jonas. He was staring in the direction of his office, an amused smile on his lips.

"Who's a pig?" Leslie asked.

"I'm not calling anybody a pig," Jonas protested. "Hell, she used to be one of my best waitresses."

"Oh, you mean Patsy." Leslie stared off at the office door now. The young mother. What had Patsy awakened within her? Were there secrets best left covered?

"She wanted to be a singer, but never quite made it." Jonas shook his head. "She was a good waitress though. Bright, cheerful. All the guys fell in love with her."

Leslie nodded her head. One of those guys apparently loved her very much, enough to make her a happy young mother.

"Then one day, this young farmer walks in. He announces that no woman of his is working in a place like this and hauls her out. I would've called the cops except she didn't fight him none."

But Leslie was barely listening. She'd been drawn to babies whenever she saw one—in the store, on walks through the park—but this was the first time she'd been able to hold one. It made her feel whole. Why? She tried to force those doors open, the memories to come forward.

"I guess it takes all kinds to make a world," Jonas said.

Leslie felt a headache coming on. From despair at not remembering, or from fear of remembering? She started toward her dressing room.

"Leslie," Jonas called after her.

Her stomach was churning. Why couldn't she remember? The doctors Jonas had sent her to said nothing was physically wrong. She'd remember when she wanted to, they all said. Well, she wanted to remember now, so why couldn't she?

Jonas came hurrying after her. "Leslie?" His voice was filled with concern. "Leslie, are you all right?"

"I have a bit of a headache." She didn't want to stop. She didn't want Jonas to see the turmoil inside her. He was so kind, so concerned about her. He'd found her collapsed from exhaustion in front of the club weeks ago and had brought her in like a stray kitten. She didn't want to give him anything else to worry about.

"Do you want me to get you anything?" he asked. "You don't have to go on tonight if you're not feeling well."

"No, I'll be fine." Maybe throwing herself into her songs would lift her spirits. "And the club is starting to fill up. We don't want to disappoint the customers."

Jonas laughed. "Don't worry about that. I'll give them all a round on the house and they'll be satisfied. I don't want you getting sick for this joint."

"I'll be fine," she assured him. "I just want to lie down for a little bit."

"Okay, kid," he said. "But remember, this ain't no slave camp."

Leslie nodded, but moved quickly away. She knew Jonas meant well, but his adoration was so open it hurt her. There was no way she could return his feelings, not that she didn't want to. She just couldn't—couldn't bring herself to open up and give. She might not remember anything of her past, but she knew that love hurt.

Jill slammed the door behind her and rushed into the kitchen. Her hands shaking, she splashed a healthy measure of vodka into a glass. The warm liquid left a searing path behind it as it tumbled down into her stomach. Once there it ignited a ball of fire.

She kicked off her shoes, put some ice in her glass, and topped off the liquid. Then she walked into the living room and sat down on the sofa. The flame still blazed in her stomach. Maybe she should have put the ice in first, but she absolutely needed that swallow.

Closing her eyes, Jill breathed deeply, forcing a picture of a mountain meadow into her mind, blue skies overhead, and an eagle lazily circling. The flame in her stomach died to embers; she felt her body relax. She took a sip from her glass, and this time a tiny tingle of warmth meandered to the very tips of her toes and fingers.

"Oh, God." She laughed aloud. "I think I've done it. I really think I've done it." Her second sip was larger, but her body was now prepared for the hot liquid.

There was only one weakness to her plan, but there was nothing she could do about it. She'd just have to tough it out. But then, no risk, no glory. No pain, no gain.

And she had a lot to gain. She was sick

and tired of her miserable existence and this crummy little apartment. She was going to have status. Status and money. She was going to be Mrs. Stuart Brooks.

As Mrs. Stuart Brooks she would have a big house, cars, furs, and jewels. She wouldn't have to work anymore and she could vacation at the best spots all over the world. She'd even get her mother out of her little house. Maybe she'd buy her a condo. That would be nice.

A sour taste bubbled up from her stomach and Jill gulped a large swallow of her vodka. Liz might have had plans for Stuart, but she hadn't acted on them. And she who hesitates loses, or something like that. This was a rough world. A person had to scratch or get left out in the cold.

Jill drained her glass. Besides, Liz wouldn't be happy as Mrs. Stuart Brooks. She believed all that stuff about the meek inheriting the earth and it being easier for a camel to pass through the eye of a needle than for a rich man to get to heaven.

Jill's living room was getting brighter and fuzzier, all at the same time, and she laughed in pure joy. She was really doing her mother a favor. If Liz had married Stuart she wouldn't be happy. All that wealth would create a load of guilt that Liz wouldn't be able to handle. The poor woman would die of depression.

Jill rattled the ice in her glass and drained the remaining drops of water. What a wonderful daughter she was. She'd take on the burdens of wealth while Liz would live out her comfortable life of sacrifice and service. She would help her mother secure her place in the hereafter.

With both hands, Jill gripped the glass until all her knuckles turned white. All these wonderful things would come to pass, just as long as Stuart didn't make that phone call.

"Jonas, Jonas," Leslie sighed as he kissed her palm. She patted his cheek gently. "It's something I have to do. It's not your problem."

He held her hand tightly. "Your problems are my problems," he said. "I want to take care of you, Leslie. Forever."

She gently pulled her hand back and wrapped her arms around herself. It was time to leave; she'd realized that in the few days since Patsy had brought her baby into the nightclub. Since holding that child in her arms, Leslie had thought of nothing else. She'd ached to hold a child again, ached to unlock the mysteries of her past.

"You don't know who I am," she told Jonas softly. "You don't know anything about me." She wanted to say she might be married, that she might have children, but she couldn't. "I don't know what I'll find."

She didn't want to find she'd hurt him.

"I'm a big boy, Leslie, and I want to go. There might be some monsters in your past. I want to make sure that they don't eat you up."

Leslie tried to smile but couldn't quite do it. Jonas was in love with her, but could she ever return his love? Was there anything in her to give?

After a long while Jonas broke the silence. "Why don't you wait until tomorrow?" he asked. "Give yourself a good night's sleep before you set off on your journey."

Leslie shook her head. "No, I'd rather get a start on things. I want to get in a hotel and then walk around Genoa City." Was she afraid that if she stayed she'd never leave? Could she stay comfortably in the shelter of Jonas's love? Why didn't she try and see?

"What are you going to be looking for?" he asked.

She shrugged her shoulders and sat on the edge of his desk. "Keys. Clues. I'll know when I see them." She dropped her hands and stretched them out in front of herself. "It's like having a vague idea where someone lives. You can't tell anyone how to get there, but once you get in the car you drive right to it."

Jonas nodded, but Leslie was sure that he really didn't understand. He wasn't the type to have emotional traumas, so how could he understand the fear she lived with each day? The agony of not knowing anything about herself. She lived in a land that he had never visited, a land that had no relationship to his world, to anyone's world.

"Well, I'd better get packed," he said. "And I have a few things to cover with Margot before we leave."

"Jonas," Leslie pleaded. "You don't have to go."

He stopped and looked at her a long moment. "Don't you want me to go?"

Leslie looked into his eyes, then had to look away from the love she saw there. "I don't know," she said, almost a whisper. "I really don't know."

Jonas came back, putting an arm around her shoulder. "I'm not worried, kid," he said. "So relax. Everything will work out for the best."

He moved away and Leslie closed her

eyes, leaning back against the desk again. Everything would work out for the best. But what was the best? And the best for whom?

Deep in her heart she just knew that everyone would not end up happy. Who would be hurt? Jonas, herself—or both? Who else was there to be hurt?

Who else was there? That was the real question. Did she have sisters, brothers? Were her parents still living? Was there a husband she loved? And would her child remember her?

Leslie wasn't surprised by the last question anymore. She was sure that she had a child and that child lived in Genoa City.

Why Genoa City, she didn't know. But there was no doubt in her mind that she had a child. There was an emptiness in her that had been just a vague feeling until Patsy had brought her baby in. That child hadn't filled Leslie's arms perfectly, but she'd almost fit. Close enough so that Leslie now knew why that void in her existed. She'd had a child. It had been taken, or given away, and now there was a void, a void that had to be filled. That was the only thing Leslie was certain of.

"I'm ready to fly, babe."

She looked up into Jonas's soft smile and concerned eyes. A pain seized her heart along with an "almost" feeling of love. That was the only way Leslie could describe it. She would have liked to love Jonas in return, but until she knew who she was it wouldn't be right. Another man might already have her heart.

"Jonas, please," she said. "I don't think you should go."

"I'm not letting you out in that world alone," he said.

Leslie looked away. "You have your business."

"No problem there," he replied. "Margot will look after it. She figures she can do a better job than me anyway."

"But—"

He put a finger to her lips. "My thoughts and my love will be with you no matter where you go," he said. "I might as well send my body along, too."

Leslie couldn't bear to look at him. He was going to get hurt. She just knew he was. It was like watching an airplane fall from the sky. You knew people would be hurt, but there wasn't a thing you could do about it. Why didn't she just stay here? Because she couldn't live with the unknown and the sense of emptiness.

24

Jonas picked up her bag. "Come, my princess," he said jovially. "Your carriage awaits thee."

Leslie glumly followed him outside. He was risking himself, and she couldn't even give him a smile.

Chapter Two

First Steps

The chimes sang out, signaling the opening of the beauty salon's door. "Damn," Derek muttered as he put the finishing touches to his tie. He should have locked the door when the last operator left, but he was in such a hurry to get home to Kay that he hadn't bothered. Well, the customer would just have to come back tomorrow.

"I'm sorry," he called out. "We're closed. Call tomorrow morning for an appointment and we'll be happy to take care of you."

"Will I need an appointment, Derek?" a voice called from near the front of the shop.

"Appointments are to everyone's advantage," he said, turning around and slipping his coat on at the same time. "You have your own time and we can schedule ourselves better." He hesitated a moment and stared at the blond young woman in front of him. It couldn't be, could it? "It makes for better service," he finished lamely.

A smirk played on her lips. "You always were good in the service department."

"Suzanne?" What would his ex-wife be doing here?

"Yes, Derek." She laughed. "Suzanne."

"I—I," he stammered. "I'm surprised. What are you doing here in Genoa City?"

Suzanne shrugged, then moved over to one of the stations. She leaned back and crossed her legs. They were as shapely as ever, but the sight didn't stir him. "My horoscope said it would be the ideal place for me."

"Your horoscope?"

"Sure," Suzanne replied. "It said I had some special friends here."

"Oh yeah? Anybody I know?"

She threw her head back with laughter. "Oh, Derek. You haven't changed a bit." Suzanne sprang up, throwing her arms around his neck. "You're my special friend." She kissed him on the lips.

"Well, uh." He gave a nervous laugh. "Actually I have changed. I'm married now."

Her arms remained around his neck,

but when he did not respond Suzanne pushed herself away. "I heard."

She walked around the work station, fingering bottles of rinse and shampoo. Then she looked in the mirror and patted her hair.

"She's an older woman, isn't she?"

Derek watched Suzanne with all the fascination of a child gazing at a cobra in the zoo. "Not that you'd notice it."

"Oh, Derek." She giggled, patting his cheek again. "I'm sure that you notice."

"The only thing I notice is that she's a lovely woman," he said. "A very lovely woman."

"Sure." Suzanne looked around the beauty shop. "Nice place. I imagine you had to save a lot of pennies for a long time to afford all of this."

Derek could feel his cheeks grow warm. "Kay thought the shop would be a good investment."

"It looks like she's getting a good return on her investment," Suzanne simpered.

The heat remained in his cheeks, but now it was fueled by anger. Suzanne had always been a spiteful bitch, but he hadn't found that out until they were married. Fortunately he was a lot smarter now. "If you want an appointment, please call tomorrow," he said brusquely. "We're closed, and I have plans for the evening."

"Poor Derek," Suzanne crooned. "Work here all day and then you have to go home to more work."

"I live in a mansion with servants," Derek snapped. "I don't have to do any work there."

"No work at all. How nice."

Derek felt a strong urge to slap Suzanne's smart mouth. "That's right, no work at all. I enjoy life with this wife. She's not bitchy and whining like some wives."

Suzanne's eyes darkened, but her voice was low and pleasant. "We were kids then. I think we've both learned a lot in the past years."

"Yes," Derek said. "I've learned what real love is."

"Derek, stop it." Suzanne's anger overflowed from her eyes to twist her face and put a snap to her words.

"I don't care whether you believe it or not," he said. "Kay and I love each other and have a wonderful life together. In fact, she's on me all the time to hire a manager for this place and spend more time with her. I may just do that."

Suzanne merely shook her head and put her smile back in place.

"Now," he said, taking her arm, "if you want an appointment, call us in the morning."

"When are you open?" The emphasis was on *you*.

He was almost dragging her to the door. "It was nice of you to visit, Suzanne, but my days are full. Between this shop and Kay, I don't have a minute to spare."

"We'll see," she said, and closed the door behind herself.

Derek locked the front door, turned off the lights, and hurried toward the back. He shook his head, laughing as he eased his Mercedes convertible out into the street. He hadn't thought Suzanne was all that great when he was a horny kid just out of high school. Now that he knew a woman like Kay, Suzanne was insignificant. He hoped she would soon tire of Genoa City and move on. He didn't need her hanging around. Derek pushed the accelerator down.

At the Chancellor mansion he bypassed the garage and parked in front of the main entrance. Let one of the servants put the car away. Why be rich if he couldn't enjoy it? The door opened before he could put a hand on it.

"Derek." Kay leapt out and devoured him in a hug. He kissed her hard. "I was worried. You've never been this late before."

"I'm sorry," he said as they walked into the house hand in hand. "Some woman tried to push in before I locked the door. I should have called, but I didn't want to waste any more time getting to you."

She laughed in her excitingly husky voice and kissed him again. "Good," she said. "Life is too short to waste."

He stopped and took Kay in his arms again. "Now that I have you, I don't want to waste a single solitary second."

They kissed long and hard, pressing their lips, and their bodies, to each other. Their hungers awoke. They broke for a second and then Kay clasped him to her again, fingers entwined in the hair on the back of his head.

"If you didn't work in that shop all day we—"

"I'm going to start looking for a manager tomorrow," he interrupted her.

Kay raised her beaming face to his, and they kissed again. "Hungry?" she asked.

"For you?" He laughed. "Always."

"Hobbs," Kay called into the dining room. "Derek and I have some very pressing business matters to discuss. Please hold dinner for a while."

The doorbell rang, and Liz Foster dabbed a last bit of Stuart's favorite perfume behind each ear, then hurried toward the door. Poor Stuart had been working so hard lately that they hadn't had a chance to see each other much since he'd returned from Las Vegas.

"Stuart, it's so good to see you."

"Liz," he responded with a curt nod.

Liz stood back to let him enter, slamming the door shut on the fluttering of concern within herself as she shut the door to her house. There couldn't be anything wrong. Stuart had been working hard and he was just tired.

"Let me take your coat," she said.

But Stuart did not remove it. "That's okay," he said. "I won't be staying long."

"You'll stay as long as you need to in order to relax."

Liz pulled the coat off his reluctant shoulders. A slight tightening in her stomach was her only concession to worry. Why would he only be staying a short time? She hadn't seen him in days. What business was so pressing that he would drop in and not remove his coat?

"Sit down," she said, "and I'll pour you some tea. I've made those cherry tarts you love so."

A fleeting expression, as if from pain, crossed his face. Maybe Stuart wasn't feeling well. Liz promised herself to have a talk with him. It was time for a man his age to start slowing down, to pause a bit and smell the roses along the way.

When she returned from the kitchen, Stuart was still standing. "Stuart, would you please sit down?"

"I really won't be staying long."

"Just sit down," Liz insisted. "Here, drink some tea, it will make you feel better."

He took the cup from her, but he just stared into it. Liz hesitated a moment, then reached for her own cup. Maybe it would help him if she started things. She took a cherry tart and bit into it.

"I have to admit"—she laughed—"these are the best ones I've made yet."

Stuart was still staring into his cup.

"I don't know where to start, Liz."

The dark cloud grew thicker, menacing her sunshine a little. Liz put her pastry down.

"They say the best place to start is at the beginning, Stuart."

He quivered sharply, as if chilled, then put both hands to his face, covering his eyes. When he let them drop, he still would not look at her.

"I can't marry you because I have to marry Jill," he said, his voice barely audible.

Liz's pain was sudden, but cloaked with confusion. "Jill who?"

His lips twisted up at the corners, but

no light of joy entered his eyes. In fact, the pain within them seemed to grow more intense.

"Jill Foster," he answered. "Your daughter."

Liz almost dropped her cup, but managed to place it on the table after spilling only a bit. Her breath was short and came with difficulty. The pounding of her heart echoed in her temples. She opened her mouth, but no words came.

"The beginning." Stuart sighed. "The beginning was my last night in Las Vegas. Jill was there."

Stuart stole a glance at Liz. Her sweet, gentle face mirrored the shock of a woman who had lost everything. How could he tell Liz that her daughter had seduced him? He wouldn't.

"We went upstairs together, and I turned into an animal."

Liz looked at him, bewilderment and questions fighting for space in her eyes. Stuart turned away even as a low moaning sound escaped her. He squeezed his eyes tightly, so tightly that not a single tear could escape. He deserved no sympathy, and certainly not from a woman like Liz.

"And now she's pregnant," he finished.

A numbness had settled over Liz, and she stared idly at the pastry lying on the table in front of her, a half-moon bite taken from its side. She ate too many sweets. They kept her plump, but sweets were one of the few things that she really enjoyed. One of the few things she had left that she enjoyed.

"Is—" Liz hesitated. She couldn't bring herself to say her daughter's name. "Is she going to keep the baby?"

Stuart nodded.

"That's good," Liz said. "I've always thought every child deserves a chance at life."

Stuart said nothing.

"A child also deserves to know its father."

"That's why I'm marrying her," Stuart replied.

Liz nodded.

The silence between them stretched out. Far in the distance Liz heard a cuckoo bird happily announce the time. She used to have a cuckoo clock. It sounded just like that. Her pain somehow didn't matter.

"You're doing the right thing, Stuart."

"I don't know," he said.

"You are," Liz insisted. "You are a decent, honorable—"

"Please, Liz." His words were an anguished cry, pleading with her. "Please don't say things like that. I don't deserve your respect."

"One mistake does not change a man," Liz answered.

Stuart sprang up and moved quickly to the window. He stood there with his back to her. Liz sat there, looking at her living room, seeing nothing. Life went on as pain and disbelief swallowed her up. She loved Stuart so much. It had seemed a miracle at first that he should love her back, but somehow the miracle had seemed real and right and likely to stay around. She should have known better.

Slowly her eyes came back to her living room. The red floral print on her sofa came into focus first, then the landscape scene on the far wall, along with the little cupid statue on her bookshelves. At length she could clearly make out Stuart's back.

"Your tea is getting cold, Stuart. Would you like me to pour you another cup?"

He turned slowly, and her heart ached for him. In the time she had been drifting, Stuart had turned into an old man. His face had grayed to match his hair. His eyes were watery and tired.

"It's best that I left," he said.

"You didn't touch your tart," Liz said. "Would you like to take some with you?"

He wiped at his eyes.

"Perhaps I'll give some to the little boy down the street, then," Liz said. "I really don't need sweets. I'm plump enough as it is."

"You're a lovely, lovely woman, Liz." His voice choked, and Liz couldn't hear his other words. He went to the closet and took out his coat. Liz walked with him to the door.

Stuart stood there a moment, his face working. Finally he took her hand and, looking at the floor, whispered, "I'm sorry." Then, quickly, he was gone.

Liz stood and stared at the closed door. What was it about her? She tried to be a good, cheerful, and interesting person. Yet, all through her life, she could never keep a man. It was always some other woman who stepped in and took her happiness. And now it was her own daughter.

"Oh, my God. Leslie?" a man whispered.

Leslie stood, staring at the man sitting alone at the small table in the corner of the restaurant. It was her first morning in Genoa City, and the memories had not come flowing back as she'd hoped. Jonas was at the library checking old newspapers while she wandered around. She'd chosen this restaurant purely by chance, or so she'd thought. The murmur of the lunch crowd flowed around her as the man stood up, coming closer to her.

"Hello, Lucas."

It was her voice. She recognized the sound and felt the air as it pushed past her voice box, but the speaker seemed to be someone else. The man was not familiar to her, but a part of her seemed to know him, and that part called him by name.

"My God, Leslie. It is you. Where have you been?"

The man seemed to know her, but he could have been mistaken. His hands were shaking, his pupils were dilated, and sweat was appearing on his brow.

"I'm hungry, Lucas." The voice was cool and calm. "May I have lunch with you?"

The man called Lucas simply nodded and helped her with a chair. Then he sat down, just staring at her.

"What are you having?" she asked him.

"A steak sandwich. The special is corned beef and cabbage."

"I don't like that much," she said, smiling at the discovery. There was so much that she didn't know about herself, but this man would help her.

"I'll have a steak sandwich also."

"Would you like anything to drink?"

"Milk," she answered.

He placed the order with the waiter and then turned to her. "Leslie, what happened? We looked everywhere for you."

Leslie frowned at the napkin she pulled from the dispenser. "I'm not sure myself," she admitted. "I haven't been able to remember anything about myself."

"Nothing?" he asked.

Leslie shook her head slowly, but was silent for a moment. He was starting to look familiar. The quiet, earnest eyes, the curled blond hair. There were other memories screaming to be let out, pounding and scratching at the doors in her mind.

Lucas folded his hands, just watching her quietly. She had to take it slowly. Very slowly, so that she didn't stumble and fall. If that happened she might be lost again, even more lost.

"Lucas Prentiss."

Lucas nodded his head. "And your name is Leslie."

"Yes, I know."

"Leslie Brooks . . . Prentiss."

She closed her eyes. There was a terrible pounding in her head. It hurt. Leslie held her eyes closed until the pain went away. When she opened them, she looked straight into Lucas's earnest blue eyes. It appeared that she had given her pain to him. She felt bad about that.

"We're . . ." She couldn't find the strength to say the words.

"Husband and wife," he finished for her.

The answer was not unexpected, but with the knowledge that Lucas was telling the truth came sorrow. Poor Jonas. How would she tell him?

"Where have you been, Leslie? How did you happen to walk in here?"

Something told her not to discuss Jonas just yet. "I came to the hotel, the one just down the street, last night. I've spent the morning walking around town. I just let my feet take me where they would. They brought me here."

"I must remember to thank your feet," Lucas said with a half smile.

"Do you eat here often?"

"Just about every day."

Their sandwiches came, and Leslie ate. She was ravenous suddenly, ready to speak only when she was finished and lingering with her milk.

"I have a father," she said.

"Yes, Stuart Brooks. He owns the newspaper here in town."

"Anybody else?" she asked.

"Your mother is dead, but you do have sisters."

Sisters. Three. "Their names are Laurie, Chris, and Peggy," she said. "What are my brothers' names?"

"You don't have any brothers."

No brothers. But who were those men? There were two of them on the far edges of her consciousness. Tall men, handsome. Was one Lucas? The pain started coming on again, and all the people shrank back. Her hands started shaking. She was going to lose her memories.

"We have a son," Lucas said.

All those clamoring people were pushed back and the doors were slammed shut. The pain left with them. Her empty yearning returned, but Leslie was comfortable. One memory remained, and her emptiness would be filled. She had a child.

"I want to see him," Leslie said. "I want to see my little Brooks."

Chapter Three

Faces from the Past

"I'm not really sure how to handle the introductions," Leslie said quietly. The two men stood glaring at each other in the hotel lobby where she and Lucas had come back to wait for Jonas. How did one introduce them? Did one introduce the boyfriend to the husband, or vice versa?

"I'm Jonas Markham."

Lucas just nodded, shaking his hand with the briefest of contact.

"I work in his nightclub," Leslie explained, then paused, trying to put her relationship with Jonas into words. "And he's a very close friend. He took care of me when I needed it."

"My name is Lucas Prentiss." Lucas's head was high, his demeanor haughty.

Leslie turned to Jonas. "Lucas says he's my husband."

"I *am* your husband."

She ignored Lucas's words. "Lucas says that I have a child," she told Jonas. "I want to see him."

"You should," Jonas said. His eyes and his voice were soft with his understanding of her pain. She gave him a tight smile, grateful for his strength through all of this.

But Lucas must have seen the exchange, brief and harmless as it was. "I'm taking Leslie to see her child," he corrected her. His tone was that of a little boy daring an adversary to cross an imaginary line.

Jonas stared at Lucas for a long moment. Leslie could see the animosity between the two men and felt saddened that she was the cause. One man was her husband, the other a dear friend. But she didn't love either of them. Did she love any man? A hazy figure loomed at the far edges of her mind, but he wouldn't come any closer.

"I'll follow you in my car," Jonas said.

Lucas led her to his car and didn't break the silence until they were on their way. After glaring in his rearview mirror, he said, "I don't like that man."

"He helped me when I needed it most," Leslie pointed out gently. She didn't want to hurt anyone else, but she didn't want to be smothered by their love either.

The silence returned and held them until Lucas parked the car.

"Your baby is with your sister."

"Laurie!"

The name popped out of her mouth. It came so quickly, without any prompting or thought, that it surprised Leslie. Suddenly page upon page of information was revealed to her. Laurie, the aggressive one. Laurie, the glamorous one. Laurie, who had studied in Paris.

Lucas had walked around to open the door for her, but as he neared the door, a sharp pain exploded in her head. Leslie put her hands to her face as more figures came forward from the murky shadows of her mind.

"Laurie's married to your brother," she whispered. "His name is Lance."

"Yes, that's right." Lucas's voice sounded as if it came from the bottom of a deep well.

"Leslie, is anything wrong?" It was Jonas's voice. She let her hands slide down and looked into his concerned eyes.

"Nothing's wrong," Lucas snapped, answering for her.

"I'm all right," she said quietly. The memories receded for the moment and she was relieved, sensing that the more she remembered, the more she would hurt. "I guess I'm just a little nervous."

Jonas put his hand out to help her from the car. "That's very understandable," he said.

"I really see no need for you to be here," Lucas told Jonas, his tone angry and petulant.

Emotions were swirling wildly in Leslie's mind. Who was who, and where did she belong? Names, faces, places were coming at her so fast she couldn't keep track of them all. She wasn't up to coping with Lucas's possessiveness or making a decision to send Jonas away. He'd been her strength through so much.

"I'll wait out here," Jonas said softly. "I'll be here if you need me."

Leslie smiled her thanks and let Lucas take her arm. They went up the sidewalk to the front door.

"What the hell makes him think anyone will need him?" Lucas muttered under his breath, but Leslie had no chance to answer, even had she wanted to. The door flew open and Laurie was standing there, staring at her.

"Leslie!" she cried. But her face was white, her tone hardly one of joy.

"Hello, Laurie," Leslie said quietly. They'd never been close, not since they were adults; she remembered that now. Laurie had always seemed to want whatever Leslie had, though that memory in itself seemed ridiculous in light of all Leslie had been through.

"What do you want?" Laurie asked.

But it was Lucas who answered, putting his hand on Leslie's back and ushering her past Laurie's unyielding frame. "Leslie's come to see little Brooks," he said.

Laurie's eyes flared with anger and pain as she spun around to face them. "Just like that?" she cried. "If that isn't just like you. Waltz off for a lifetime, then waltz back when you choose."

Leslie was stunned by her sister's attack, by the hatred and bitterness in Laurie's voice.

"It wasn't like that at all," Lucas snapped. "Leslie was in an accident. She had amnesia and couldn't come back to us."

Laurie's face didn't soften, but she turned on her heel. "The nursery's down here."

Leslie followed slowly, grateful that Lucas seemed prepared to wait in the living room. She wasn't sure why, but she knew this reunion was private and had nothing to do with Lucas. A strange certainty, she thought, about the man who claimed to be her husband.

The nursery was picture perfect, its yellow walls decorated with rainbows and balloons. It shone with happiness and with love, the kind of nursery Leslie would have wanted for her baby. The knowledge hurt as she inched forward to the crib.

The baby was beautiful, gurgling and kicking his feet as he looked up at her and smiled a wide toothless grin. A ball of sunshine exploded within her as a deep, overpowering love shook her to the core. This was her child.

"He's beautiful," she said softly, tears of joy trickling down her cheeks.

Laurie said nothing, but didn't stop Leslie as she reached down to pick up her son. He slipped into the nook of her arms like a lost lamb cuddles up to its mother. It felt so good and so natural. His little hand closed around her finger.

"Please be careful," Laurie said. "He's just getting over a cold and tires easily."

Leslie kissed Brooks on the forehead, then laid him gently back in the crib. "Go to sleep, sweetheart," she whispered. "Go to sleep. Mommy's here now."

Leslie looked up to find Laurie's gaze icy and intense. "As far as he knows, his mother has always been here," she snapped.

Leslie looked into her sister's face and tried to read what she saw there. Fear? Pain? Hate? All of the above? Leslie felt herself grow weary, very weary. Her arms ached to hold her child, but she didn't have the strength to fight at the moment.

"Did you want anything else?" Laurie asked. "My home? My husband?"

Leslie turned on leaden feet and walked out of the nursery. In the foyer she looked from the pain in Laurie's face to the obvious concern in Lucas's. Weariness and confusion rode her shoulders.

"I'd like to leave now," she told Lucas.

Once they were out, Lucas put his arm around her. It was another weight on her shoulders, but she was too tired to throw it off.

That baby was certainly hers, but was this man the father? That other figure darted around the shadows of her mind again. He was blurred, but Leslie could see his lips move. Yet no sound came.

Who was her child's father? She wanted to stand on the highest tower in Genoa City and scream the question, but she feared that Lucas would be the only one who came forward.

"Leslie, are you all right?"

Leslie left the shelter of Lucas's arm and fell into the comfort of Jonas's embrace. "It's my baby," she said.

His only reply was to pat her on the back softly, as a mother did for a baby, but her pain was too deep to be soothed away.

"Leslie, let me take you home."

It was Lucas, but Leslie didn't want to leave the security of Jonas's arms. She couldn't bring herself to respond in any way.

"Leslie." His voice was pleading. "Everything in our home is just the way you left it."

"Back off." Leslie heard Jonas's voice rumble from deep in his chest. "Give her some room. Leslie's had a lot of things come flying at her today."

"I can get a doctor, Leslie."

"She's going back to her hotel room," Jonas said.

"Hotel room!" Lucas exclaimed. "Absolutely not. I forbid it."

"Who the hell cares?"

Leslie lifted her head from Jonas's chest. She couldn't handle verbal violence right now, so she surely couldn't cope with anything physical between the two of them.

"Look, I—"

But Jonas interrupted her. "The hotel room is neutral ground," he said. "Go there and lie down. When you're all rested, then start sorting things out."

That made sense. Leslie nodded her head, letting Jonas lead her to his car. She knew that Lucas was still there, but she couldn't find the strength to say good-bye as Jonas opened the car door, tenderly helping her into the seat. He looked crestfallen as he slowly made his way to the driver's side. Silently he started the car and left the driveway.

He let his reflexes drive the car while he sat with his depression in a far dark corner. He knew that it wouldn't have been right to deny Leslie her past. Her past was a big part of who she was, but he had never expected something like this.

A boyfriend, even a husband. Jonas had prepared himself for the likelihood of either. After all, Leslie was one fine lady, and she would have had to spend her life in a cave not to have one or the other. But a kid. A baby of her own.

He'd been all set to compete, but there was no way he could compete with a baby. He feared her past had claimed her.

Suzanne ground out her cigarette in the smoked-glass ashtray. Where was that woman? Maybe senility had already overtaken the wonderful Kay and she couldn't find the restaurant.

She drained her glass and signaled the waiter for another. Boy, that woman sure had Derek jumping through a hoop. But the little boy always did like his candy and toys, and that old mama had plenty of

sugar. She could buy her little boy anything his heart desired. A Mercedes convertible. A beauty shop of his own and
good people to run it for him. A mansion
with a swimming pool.

The waiter brought her drink and
Suzanne gulped at it. Derek wasn't as
bold as he used to be, either. He wasn't
about to do anything to make mama bear
angry with him. A boy scout didn't have
anything on Derek. Poor Derek acted
more like a Trappist monk.

"Miss Lynch?"

Startled, Suzanne looked up at the regal
woman standing before her.

"Yes."

"I'm Kay Thurston. You invited me to
lunch."

A tightness took over all of Suzanne's
body. Her jaws clenched, her hand
squeezed the liquor glass, and her stomach tried a simple square knot. The
woman looked even younger up close.

Suzanne forced a smile to her lips and
the worrisome thoughts from her mind.
"Yes," she said. "How good of you to
come. Sit down, please."

Kay sat down and then, before Suzanne
could summon the waiter, snapped her
fingers.

"I'd like a Bloody Mary."

The waiter made a short bow and was gone. Suzanne couldn't help but admire the woman. She'd never even looked up to see if the man was there, just assuming that he would be—and he was. It was as if she'd willed it.

Suzanne used the few minutes of silence, while they waited for Kay's drink, to collect herself. Kay looked good because of the marvels of plastic surgery, Suzanne told herself. And she probably came to this restaurant often, so the waiters all knew her. Nothing special. Just a long-time Genoa City dowager.

"Madam."

Kay reached for her drink and took a sip. Again, she didn't bother to look at the waiter or acknowledge him in any way.

"What brings you to our fair city?"

Suzanne had had her mouth open, but Kay spoke first. Damn. The woman was her luncheon guest and now she was making out like she owned the whole city.

"I'm heading east," Suzanne said. "But Wisconsin is so pretty this time of the year that I thought I'd visit for a while."

"How nice," Kay purred.

Suzanne tried to sip her drink and then found herself rattling the ice cubes in the otherwise empty glass.

"Would you like another?" Kay asked.

"No," Suzanne said, forcing a decisive tone into her voice. "Let's order our food."

Kay didn't bother to reach for her menu. "Do you like fish?" she asked. "Their whitefish in cream sauce is sinfully delicious."

"No, I don't like fish." Suzanne studiously perused the menu.

"The turkey tetrazzini is good. If you like, I'll speak to the waiter and make sure that Pierre cooks the pasta al dente. I just hate it when the noodles lie on your plate, lifeless. Don't you?"

"I'll have the filet and a baked potato."

Kay raised an eyebrow, then, shrugging, she snapped her fingers for the waiter.

"I'm not into fancy foods," Suzanne said, satisfied to be first to throw her words into the waves of silence the waiter left in his wake. "I like food plain, but substantial."

"Hmm," was Kay's only reply.

"That's why I enjoyed Derek so much." Suzanne smiled. Kay didn't change her bored expression, but Suzanne could see that she had winced. It certainly wasn't a mortal blow, but she had scored points.

Like a wolf sensing blood, Suzanne moved in on her opponent. "Most days I wouldn't go out for lunch," she said. "That was my only chance to sleep, undisturbed. Derek wouldn't leave me alone." She paused for effect. "But then such diversions do have a way of making the night go by."

Kay smiled. "Young men do have a voracious appetite," she said. "It isn't until they mature a bit that they develop any taste."

The heat slowly climbed up her neck as if she were a thermometer. Suzanne hoped that her face wouldn't get red. That old lady was certainly a sneaky bitch. Suzanne gratefully turned her attention to the meal being put before her. They ate in silence.

As they neared the end of the luncheon Suzanne quickly swallowed the last of her food. She could control the waiter as well as Kay. All she had to do was go first.

"Would you care for any dessert?" she asked as she snapped her fingers for the waiter.

"No, thank you," Kay replied. "I have mine at home."

Suzanne's jaw clenched shut, like a steel trap. The waiter stood looking at her, waiting for a command.

"Would you care for a Drambuie?" Kay asked.

The best Suzanne could do was shake her head. Kay then raised one finger to the waiter and smiled.

He quickly brought Kay her drink, clearing the table before he left. Kay sipped at the liqueur and smiled blandly. Suzanne felt her luncheon sitting in her stomach like a load of cement, control slipping from her fingers. It was certainly time to stop being respectful to her elders.

"Derek used to be such a physical man," Suzanne said, arching her eyebrows. "We had great times swimming, hiking, playing softball, and all kinds of things."

"He hasn't lost any of his energy," Kay said. "We've scuba dived in the Caribbean, rafted down the Colorado, and this winter we'll ski the Alps."

Suzanne put her hands under the table and clenched them together. "Derek always liked that I could keep up with him."

"Oh, really?" Kay sipped her drink. "It just goes to show you how people change. He tells me that he enjoys the challenge of trying to keep up with me."

Even clenched together, Suzanne's hands began to quiver. That bitch. That pompous bitch. Suzanne took a deep breath and signaled the waiter.

"May I have the check, please?"

"Oh, don't worry yourself about such a little thing, Suzanne. Put it on my account, young man."

"Yes, ma'am," the waiter replied and quickly left.

Kay rolled the sweet liqueur around in her mouth and then let it slowly trickle down her throat. She was aware of the thin woman across from her and her tense eyes, but she didn't bother looking at her. Suzanne provided some mild amusement, but she certainly was no challenge.

"Well, it was certainly nice to have this chat with you."

"Mmm." Kay's eyes swept the dining room. There wasn't anyone of interest here. Anyone who was somebody ate in the series of small dining rooms in back.

"If you want any hints about handling Derek, just give me a call."

"Thank you for the offer," Kay said, still not looking at the woman. "But I prefer discovering things on my own."

They sat in silence, and Kay wondered if she was going to have to dismiss the girl.

"I understand you have quite a house," Suzanne said.

"It has its good points."

"I've never seen a real mansion before."

Kay finally looked at Suzanne. A tense little mouse of a woman, so lacking in confidence. But then, she had nothing to be confident about.

"Call my butler," Kay said. "He'll schedule a tour for you." She gathered her purse and her wrap. "I must be going now."

Suzanne stood up also. "It was nice meeting you. I'm glad we had this lunch together."

"That's good," Kay replied and then turned to leave. Actually Kay had expected that it would be more fun than it had been. It was too bad that this Suzanne person hadn't had a bit more spirit.

Suzanne stared at the departing figure. She had been concerned about her face coloring, but Suzanne knew from experience that was no longer a problem. Her face would be pale now—white hot to match her fury.

"Hello, Stuart. Please come in," Jill said, putting on her widest smile as she stood back from the door. How nicely he was coming to heel!

"I just came over to tell you to go ahead and plan the wedding," he said without a break in the frost in his eyes. "If you need any help with the scheduling, feel free to consult my secretary."

Her laugh was short and harsh. "I thought you older men were more into romance and that kind of thing," Jill said.

"You're getting a wedding ring and a father for the child you're carrying. Nothing more."

Jill heard the sound of a door closing down the hall from them and waved her hand. "I'm really not interested in discussing our personal affairs out here where everyone can hear," she said. "Won't you please come in?"

He hesitated for the longest moment. Then, setting his jaw so hard that the muscles popped in his temples, he marched into Jill's apartment.

"Would you like a drink?"

"No, thank you," he replied.

"Well, I would." She went into the kitchen and mixed herself an old-fashioned, then came back and sat down. "You can play statue if you like," she said. "But I'm going to be comfortable."

He remained standing.

"Stuart, you're bugging me. Sit down."

He surveyed the small apartment, then chose a straight-backed chair off to the corner. Jill had to turn to see him. He sat, and Jill sipped.

"Do you have any ideas for the wedding?" Jill asked.

"You have the gall to ask me?" he snorted.

Jill stared into her drink. She wasn't expecting hugs and kisses, but a little civility certainly wouldn't be out of line.

"I've talked to your mother," Stuart said. "She was very understanding."

If he didn't have to be polite, then neither did she. See how he liked a taste of his own medicine! "That's her thing," Jill said flippantly. "She's been doing it for so long that she's an expert."

Jill watched his face grow red, but then it faded back. The old man was riding for a massive coronary if he kept all his feelings bottled up like that. Not that she cared, as long as he had it after the wedding. She could spend his money without him. Stuart started to rise from his chair.

"Where are you going?" she asked. "I thought we were supposed to plan our wedding."

"I said you can plan it," he said, standing.

"I may be the star of the show"—she laughed—"but I'm not the only one on stage. I'd like some idea of what you want."

He stared at her. "I can't believe your nerve. You know damn well what I want."

Jill gulped at her drink. *Yeah. Marry sweet, understanding Liz. Fat chance, bozo.* "So it's all up to me?"

"That's right." He put his hat on.

"Okay," Jill said. "High noon at the cathedral. Then a big, huge reception at the civic club. About five or six hundred of our nearest and dearest friends."

His face turned ashen. "Surely you wouldn't do that," he said. "Not even you would do a thing like that."

"Afraid to spend the money, honey?"

"I don't give a damn about the money," he shouted. "I'm concerned about the propriety of it. I'm concerned about your mother's feelings."

"You want something a little smaller?" She laughed.

"Very small and very inconspicuous."

She shrugged. "How about a justice of the peace in Bartellston?"

"Fine." He put his hat back on. "Don't bother seeing me out," he said. "I know the way." He slammed the door behind him.

A depression mixed with anger started to settle over Jill, but she pushed the dark cloud away. She didn't want a loving husband. She wanted, and was getting, something much better. She was being freed from her constant concerns about money. No more scrimping and pinching pennies. She was going to be Mrs. Stuart Brooks.

Chapter Four

Loving Claims

"Hello, Laurie," Leslie said softly. "Thank you for letting me come over."

Her sister shrugged, then turned and walked back into her home. Leslie stepped inside and shut the door. It seemed quiet inside, too quiet, as if everything there were holding its breath and waiting to see what Leslie wanted. She shook off her nervous imaginings and followed Laurie into a small den.

"You have a very nice home," Leslie said, sitting down on the sofa across from her sister.

"Thank you," Laurie murmured. Then, after sitting through a long, painful silence, she asked, "Would you like anything to drink? Coffee or tea?"

Leslie looked down at the floor. "No, nothing, thank you."

The silence swept over them again.

"You're the one who said you wanted to talk," Laurie pointed out after a moment.

Leslie nodded and tried to gather her strength to make her speech. "This isn't going to be easy for me," she said.

Laurie chose not to help her, giving her a stony stare instead, as if she knew what Leslie was going to say.

Swallowing hard, Leslie tried again. "You've taken very good care of little Brooks."

This time Laurie only nodded her thanks.

"But I think—" Leslie jumped from her seat, unable to look at her sister any longer. She went to the window, staring out at the trees on the far edge of the property. Her palms were wet with sweat and her stomach hurt almost as badly as her labor pains had, but this had to be done.

"I'd like Brooks to come back to live with me."

Leslie's voice sounded loud in the stillness of the room. Overly loud and belligerent, which wasn't how she'd wanted to say it at all. But even so, she was able to breathe again now that it was out in the open. She'd said it, she'd finally said it. The tension and pain left her body and she waited, tensed, for the explosion. When none came, she turned slowly around. Laurie was still sitting, her hands clasped in her lap, staring at the floor.

"Laurie," Leslie said quietly. There was no response. Tension and pain began creeping back. She'd known Laurie wouldn't give in easily. "Laurie, he is my child."

"Your child? Your child?" Laurie's voice was a thin whisper, but filled with anger and bitterness.

"Yes," Leslie snapped, tension making her voice curt even though she understood Laurie's pain. She understood it, but it changed nothing. Brooks still belonged with his mother, his real mother. "He came from my body. He's blood of my blood and flesh of my flesh."

"He's a human being, Leslie. Not a bundle of flesh and blood. He has a soul. He feels, he laughs, he cries. He likes to be hugged. If it wasn't for my love, he would have died."

Guilt suddenly overwhelmed Leslie and squeezed her so that she could barely breathe. "Laurie, I'm well aware of all you've done for Brooks. I can't ever thank you enough, but he is my child and I need him."

"You need him." Laurie spat out the words. "And have you ever considered what he needs?"

"Yes," Leslie shouted. "He needs his mother."

"He has a mother."

Leslie stared into the rigid face of her sister. She had considered the possibility that Laurie would refuse to give up Brooks. But considering the possibility and staring its reality in the face were two different things.

"Laurie, please. You can visit him any time you want. You are his aunt."

"I've been a mother to him longer than you have."

"But you're *not* his mother," Leslie screamed at her sister. Her head was starting to hurt, and she turned back to the window. She was starting to lose control; she didn't want to do that. So much depended on her. Little Brooks depended on her.

"Are you going to give up your concert career?" Laurie asked. "Are you going to live here in Genoa City? Are you going to stay with Lucas?"

Laurie was taunting her, baiting her with a past that Leslie still only vaguely remembered. "Stop it," she cried. "Stop it." She covered her ears with her hands, clenching her teeth until the urge to shed tears had past; then she turned to face Laurie.

"I haven't thought everything through yet," Leslie admitted. "Just that I love my son and want him with me."

Laurie looked at her coldly, then stood up as if the sight was more than she could take. "Leslie," she said sharply. "Brooks isn't a teddy bear or a doll that we fought over when we were children. He's a child. And like every child he needs constant loving care."

"I know that," Leslie snapped back. "I'm not a child anymore. I'm an adult."

"A healthy, functioning adult?"

Leslie turned back to the window.

"What happens to Brooks if you get another one of your amnesia spells?" Laurie prodded. "Who takes care of him then?"

Leslie's head throbbed like it never had before. No, they weren't children any longer. Their fights were much crueler and much more vicious. And their mother wasn't there to have them make up, then have milk and cookies together. She almost wished she were a child again. The world seemed so much nicer then. But that was the world she had to make for her child. With new strength, she turned to her sister.

"Laurie," she said quietly. "I appreciate everything you've done for me and for

Brooks, but I must have him back. I am his mother."

"I'm his mother," Laurie said stubbornly.

"I gave him life."

"I gave him love."

"Without me, he wouldn't be here."

"Without me, he wouldn't be healthy," Laurie said. "Without me, he wouldn't be happy and smiling."

They stared at each other, then Leslie slowly walked back to the foyer. At the front door, she stopped and turned to face Laurie.

"I will stop at nothing to get my son back," Leslie said. "I'll take you to court if I have to."

"Lance and I won't give him up," Laurie said.

"Lance?" A stab of fear seemed to grab her lungs, twisting them so that Leslie couldn't breathe. She'd heard the name before and knew he was Lucas's brother and Laurie's husband, but somehow, when Laurie said it, Leslie suddenly saw a face, a body that was attached to the name.

"Yes, Lance. My husband." Laurie paused, her eyes filled with unreadable emotions, then went on. "Brooks's father."

Momentum carried Leslie through the door, but once it closed behind her, she sank inside herself, tormented with agonizing fears and uncertainties. My God, how could it be? Was Lance, her sister's husband, really her son's father?

"And do you have anybody to stand up for you?" the justice of the peace asked as a hacking cigarette cough seized him. "Allergies," he mumbled in between clearing his throat.

Jill wrinkled her nose. Maybe the man's allergy would clear up if he restricted the barley and malt he put into his system.

"Anyways," the man said, rubbing his nose with his shirt cuff. "Do you have anybody to—"

"No, we don't," Stuart snapped.

"That'll be ten dollars extra."

"I don't care."

Stuart sounded weary, and Jill was on edge. The treasure was almost hers. Just a few more inches and she would hold Stuart's wealth and social position as her own.

The justice dialed a number, then waited. "Ben," he said without introduction. "Send Wanda and Ralph over."

"You sure you don't want the deluxe?" he said, looking up as he replaced the receiver. "We got one of them little Jap organs. You know, all electric. The missus plays it real nice."

"Come on, Stuart," Jill coaxed, laughing. "It would put a little life in this affair."

Stuart threw a number of bills on the desk. "Here," he said. "Do whatever the hell you want, just make it quick."

The justice made a sound somewhere between a chuckle and a cough. "I can understand you being anxious and all," he said, flashing his nicotine-stained teeth. "You got yourself a real good-looking filly here." Neither of them responded, and he started pulling a box from his desk. "You folks need wedding rings? I got some nice ones here. Pure gold."

"No, thank you," Jill said. "We have our own."

That was one thing she hadn't backed off on. With Stuart moping and sulking ever since he'd agreed to marry her, there'd been a number of things that she hadn't pressed for, such as a reception or a church wedding, but she'd made him buy her a wedding ring. She hauled him down to the jeweler's one evening and picked out one of the best rings in stock. Gold with a number of diamonds. It was a ring that would properly reflect her new status.

"You sure you don't want to take a look at them?" the man pressed. "Wouldn't hurt. Might find something you like better."

"I doubt that," Jill said.

"Hey," the justice said with a shrug. "You don't often get pure gold at my prices."

No, only in a cereal box, Jill thought with a smirk.

The buzzer sounded behind them, indicating that someone had opened the front door. The justice hopped up. "Let me go get the missus, and we'll get this show on the road."

Jill turned to look at the man and woman who had just entered. She wore a pink waitress outfit, bouffant hairstyle, and a broad smile. Her companion wore a dark suit coat with a white T-shirt, stained white pants, and a dour expression.

"Hi," the woman said.

The man just nodded.

Stuart ignored them both, while Jill gave them a nod with a half smile.

"That's a real cute outfit," the woman said.

"Thank you," Jill murmured.

"I really love white for a bride," she gushed on. "I mean so many girls, they come in here wearing any old thing. Why, Ralph and I stood up here, I think it was a couple of weeks ago, and the woman wore red. You remember that, don't you, sweetie?'' The man did not respond in any way. "I mean, can you believe it?''

Stuart continued staring at the wall in front of him, his face like one of the visages on Mount Rushmore. Jill looked around the room, hoping the woman could take a hint.

"I mean, how can you have a wedding without the bride in white?'' she continued. "And it don't matter none how many times you done it. Every wedding should be special. Otherwise, why bother?''

"This way, folks.''

Jill followed the justice quickly, and even Stuart seemed anxious for things to get under way. An adequate representation of the wedding march greeted them.

The justice gave one last cough, clearing his nose and throat. "Wanda, you stand by the lady, and Ralph, you get over here by the fella. Sir, you want to give old Ralph here your rings?''

Stuart stared at the man, looking as though he'd rather give up his eyeteeth.

"Well, I guess you really don't have to,'' the justice said. He pulled out a tattered Bible, but a coughing spasm temporarily halted things again. "Allergies,'' he mumbled, after again clearing his nose and throat. "Well, ain't none of us getting any younger.'' He opened the small book.

"Dearly beloved,'' he mumbled. "We

71

are gathered here this day to join—" He looked at his form. "Stuart Brooks and Jill Foster in holy matrimony. If there be anyone present who objects to this union, let him speak now or forever hold his peace."

He looked up and snickered. "I ain't never lost one yet," he said.

"Do you—" He looked at his form again. "Stuart Brooks, take Jill Foster as your lawfully wedded wife? Do you promise to love, honor, and cherish her for better and for worse, for richer or poorer, in sickness and in health, until death do you part?"

Stuart stared straight ahead at the wall behind the justice.

"Sir?"

Jill poked an elbow into Stuart's ribs.

"I do," he replied through clenched teeth.

"And do you—" He checked his form. "Jill Foster, take Stuart Brooks as your lawfully wedded husband? Do you promise to love, honor, and obey him for better or for worse, for richer or poorer, in sickness and in health until death do you part?"

"I do." Her voice was strong and clear.

"Sir," the justice said. "You're going to have to give her the ring now."

Stuart's hand trembled, but the ring slid on easily and smoothly. Jill stared at the flashing diamonds, almost screaming with joy. She had it all now. Respect, position, and money. No one in Genoa City could ever look down on her again.

The man's intonations sounded mute and distant. "By the power vested in me by the state of Wisconsin, I hereby pronounce you man and wife. You may now kiss the bride."

Stuart stood still.

"Sir," the justice prompted. "You don't have to, but most people do."

Jill moved her head to kiss him on the lips and a momentary shiver of fear ran through her. Kissing Stuart was like kissing a stone in the middle of a Wisconsin winter.

"Well, good luck to you all," Wanda sang out cheerfully as Ralph pulled her through the door, but Jill was concentrating on her ring. Stuart could be as cold as he liked; his ring and his money would be warm.

"Did you tell him that it was Suzanne?"

"Yes, I did," the voice replied with a professional pleasantness.

Suzanne gripped the receiver so hard her hand hurt. "Well, tell him again," she demanded. "Tell him it's Suzanne. And just in case he doesn't know which Suzanne, tell him it's his ex-wife."

"Just a moment."

The receptionist's pleasantness was wearing thin around the edges, and Suzanne's patience was totally gone. She lit a cigarette while she waited.

"I'm sorry," the woman said. "But Derek is busy at the moment with a customer. He really can't come to the phone. He'll call you when he's free."

"He's been giving me that bullcrap for over a week now," Suzanne shouted. "I've been calling Derek all week and he's never returned my calls. I know he has my number."

"I'm sure he has, sweetheart." Before Suzanne could recover from the cutting edge in the woman's voice, she'd hung up.

"Fool," she screamed, slamming the phone down. "We'll see how smart you are when you're out on the street."

Suzanne went to the kitchenette and poured herself a gin, straight up. She wasn't going to be able to do anything if Derek never called. Bastard. He had a rich mama now who could tie his shoes and wipe the spit off his face, so he thought he didn't need Suzanne anymore.

Throwing herself into an overstuffed

chair, she swallowed another mouthful of the fiery liquid. *Face it, kid. Derek's not going to leave of his own accord.* He wasn't the smartest guy in the world, but he recognized a sweet deal when he had it. No, if she wanted Derek, Suzanne knew she'd have to knock Kay out of the box. She drained the glass, but there wasn't enough there to warm the chill that danced up and down her spine.

Suzanne looked at her empty glass. It would take a lot more than a glass of gin to give her enough courage to tackle Kay head on. Damn. That woman was tough as nails.

The left side of her stomach entered into a tug-of-war with the right side. Angry and frustrated, Suzanne threw her glass against the wall. Even that wasn't satisfying, because the glass was plastic. Nothing was satisfying in her world anymore.

Suzanne thought back to her luncheon with Kay and almost cried. That old woman was so sure of herself. Suzanne knew that Kay was older, but Kay didn't appear to be aware of it. She'd sat there looking cool, calm, and collected. Suzanne could hear her teeth grind. And beautiful. Damn it. As much as she hated to, she had to admit it. The old lady was one good-looking broad.

Suzanne kicked her shoes off, leaning back in the chair. The queen would have to be knocked off her throne. Derek had to be shown that mama had flaws and weaknesses. But how?

Her head was starting to ache, and Suzanne rubbed her eyes. She could have another drink, but she really needed something with a little more punch to it. Something that could really pick her up. Grass, or a little hash. She wondered where the local candy store was located.

Suddenly a light flashed in her consciousness. A smile slowly spread across her face. She went to her phone and quickly dialed a number in Madison. The number was etched in her brain. She chewed her lip as the phone rang. *Oh please, please let him be there.*

"Hello."

The voice was low and masked, as if there was a handkerchief over the mouthpiece.

"Barney?"

"Who's this?" There was an edge to the voice.

"Hey, Barney," she said. "This is Suzanne."

"Suzanne?"

"Yeah," she snapped. "Don't be so damn paranoid. We met last year at Columbia."

"Yeah?" More of his defenses were coming down, and the voice was brighter.

"You remember that party where Lou and Carl spiked the punch with some acid. Boy, wasn't that a gas?"

"Yeah, yeah." He chuckled. "That was really off the wall, far out."

"That was really something."

Suzanne let the silence settle among them. "People don't seem as much fun anymore," she said after a moment.

"Yeah."

"You know, I'd like to give a party and I'd like to liven it up."

"Yeah?"

"There any good acid around anymore?" Suzanne asked.

"Yeah."

"I don't think there is in Genoa City."

"Genoa City," Barney snorted. "Them farmers there get high on milk."

"You know what I think would be neat?" She didn't wait for an answer. "To take some LSD and put it in some candy. Then pass it around and stand back." She giggled.

"Yeah!"

"I don't know where to get the acid, though," she said. "I need good stuff, not some garbage like they give white rats at the med school."

"It can be done."

"And it's gotta be in good candy. You know. Swiss chocolates. That kind of stuff."

"That can be done too, but it'll cost you."

Suzanne chewed on her thumb. This was the part that worried her. What if the price was too high? She wanted Derek back, but she only had a certain amount of cash available at the moment. "How much?"

"Three hundred Georges."

She could handle that, she realized, breathing a sigh of relief. "You got it, Barney."

"Pick it up tomorrow. You spring for lunch."

The line went dead, and Suzanne hung up, giggling. Excitement bubbled within her and she danced around the room. Oh, this was going to be neat. And so easy. Go in, lick the old lady's feet, give her a little present, and zap. Zombieville.

She stopped and poured herself another drink. "Here's to us," she said, saluting a vision. "You and me, Derek. You and me."

Chapter Five

Visits

"Oh, Kay," Suzanne exclaimed. "Your home is just so lovely."

The woman reminded Kay of a field mouse as she darted about the foyer peering first in one room and then another. Small, intense, with beady, greedy eyes.

"And it's not just the large rooms and expensive furnishings," Suzanne continued. "I mean, the good taste is really obvious. That's something you can't buy."

"You can buy anything," Kay said. "If you have enough money."

Suzanne glanced at Kay, then quickly turned her attention to the long winding staircase. Kay found it so amusing watching the poor little woman trying to hide the greed and envy in her eyes.

"Thanks for letting me come over," Suzanne said. "I've seen your place a

79

number of times from the road, but I never dreamed that I'd get inside."

Kay wondered what Suzanne was doing along the road, a seldom-traveled cul de sac. It was certainly obvious that the little field mouse didn't travel in the same circles as Kay and her neighbors, so it wasn't as though she'd be invited to tea or a pool party. She was probably riding around, hoping to catch a glimpse of Derek.

Kay's lips turned up in a smile as she chuckled at the thought of the intense little woman driving around the estate country looking for her ex-husband, but then, one had to give Suzanne credit for her persistence. A lot of women would just quit and sit in a corner whining.

"Why don't we go out on the patio?" Kay suggested. "I'll have Hobbs bring us something to drink."

"Okay," Suzanne said brightly.

Leading the way, Kay was tempted to take Suzanne in hand. Someone really should. The woman needed to smooth out her emotions a bit. Right now she looked like some high school girl taking a tour of some screen idol's mansion.

"Oh," Suzanne said in almost a moan as they went outside and the gardens lay before them. "This is really beautiful. How many gardeners does it take to keep this place up?"

Kay shrugged. "I don't concern myself with those things. That's my butler's responsibility." She pressed a button beneath one of the tables, and Hobbs appeared as they were seating themselves.

"Madam?"

"I'll have a martini," Kay told Hobbs. "Make it extra dry."

"And madam's guest?" Hobbs asked. "What will she have?"

"I'll have the same thing," Suzanne responded eagerly.

"Very good, madam."

As befitted his station, Hobbs never bothered looking at Suzanne, even as he returned to serve their drinks.

"Did you inherit all this?" Suzanne asked as she leaned back, sipping at her drink and staring at the sweeping vista of grounds beyond the pool.

"I inherited this home," Kay replied. "And a number of business properties. I've greatly improved the value and profitability of those business properties."

"I would have guessed as much," Suzanne said. "You're a very competent woman."

Kay sipped her drink rather than replying.

"You're not just competent, you're also

very glamorous. Especially for someone your age."

Kay looked at her, amusement tugging at the corners of her mouth.

"I don't mean to say that you're an old lady," Suzanne added, turning and wiggling her body almost like a puppy wanting to please. "You're just maintaining a beauty that you've always had."

As she crossed her legs, Kay looked down. She was sorely tempted to remove her shoe just to see if the fawning Suzanne would fall down and kiss her foot.

"Neither Derek nor I grew up in anything like this."

Kay's smile broadened. Now they would get to the subject at hand. "Is that right? He's adjusting quite well to a life of luxury."

Suzanne played with the ribbon of a gift-wrapped box that she had brought with her. It was her only sign of agitation. She was an amateur at gamesmanship, Kay thought, but she was working hard at it. Kay admired that.

"In fact," Kay said. "Because of his background, I think Derek appreciates the things I give him more than a number of the men I have known."

Suzanne took her hand from the beribboned box and sipped her drink. She was controlling herself very well under trying circumstances.

"I do enjoy having him," Kay said. "He brings the enthusiastic joy of a little boy along with his obviously male attributes. A very nice combination."

Kay finished her drink, then licked her lips as she stared at Suzanne. She was curious as to how the little field mouse would respond.

"I wouldn't have any trouble adjusting to something like this," Suzanne said. She turned and looked at Kay. The hunger in her eyes was as raw and obvious as that of a starving dog. "And if I ever got it, I would show my appreciation every minute of every day."

Kay looked away. Maybe the woman didn't want Derek. Maybe she just wanted a life of luxury. That would certainly be a logical and intelligent choice.

"I'll keep that in mind," Kay said quietly.

"Thank you," Suzanne murmured, then sprang up. "Goodness, look at the time. I really have to be going."

Smiling, Kay rose to her feet. "So nice of you to come," she said. The woman was an obvious sycophant, but she was amusing, which was more than Kay could say for a lot of her friends.

"Thanks for having me," Suzanne said.

"I hope you'll accept this as a small token of my appreciation."

Kay laughed. "I love gifts." And she did. Like a little girl, and especially if they were wrapped. She unwrapped the paper, then squealed in delight. "Oh, Bollier's Chocolate Cremes. They are absolutely my very favorite."

Suzanne's whole face brightened. "I did so hope that you would like them," she said. "I understand that this comes from an extra-special batch."

Maybe Suzanne wasn't such a bad person after all, Kay thought. A little weak or maybe just a little unlucky. "Would you like a piece?" Kay asked.

"No! No!" Suzanne said. "I was always told that it was bad manners to eat or drink your own gift."

"Good." Kay laughed. "Then I will have them for myself. Of course, you already know that Derek doesn't like chocolate at all."

"No, I didn't," Suzanne lied.

"Strange," Kay said, shaking her head, not really paying attention to Suzanne's words. "I'd always thought that all little boys loved chocolate."

"There's no accounting for tastes," Suzanne said. "Well, I have to go. See you around."

"We certainly will." Then with a quick

wink, Kay added, "I'll look hard, my dear. Maybe I can find a wealthy old man for you."

Suzanne just waved. "I'll let myself out."

Kay put her feet up on another chair and stretched. Poor little Suzanne. A weak little thing, certainly not to be trusted, but so servile, so amusing.

Kay looked at her watch. Derek should be home soon. At first she had found his compulsion to go to his shop every day cute, but now she was starting to find it annoying. She needed him home right now. Seeing Suzanne and her funny little groveling had excited her.

The colorful box caught her eye. A piece of chocolate was no match for a firmly muscled young man, but it was better than nothing. She pulled off the cover. Her mouth watered. How lovely. Three rows of luxuriously rich dark chocolates.

Biting into the piece, she grunted happily. Kay had never understood Derek's aversion to such a delectable item. Chocolate was indeed a gift from the gods.

She ate the candy with delight, then considered another piece, but Derek would be home soon and she thought she'd take a bath first, a warm soaking one with a perfumed, bubbly soap. Derek liked it when she smelled nice.

Taking the box with her, Kay went into the house. At the top of the stairs she had to stop to catch her breath. Her head felt a trifle woozy and tiny blue spots floated in front of her eyes. She shook her head. That was a strange way to feel after only one drink.

As she entered her bedroom suite, Kay considered lying down. The floor seemed to be tilting and pitching every which way. It was like walking in the fun house, only it was all in slow motion.

"Ridiculous," she snapped, then stared in surprise at her clothes scattered on the floor. She was stark naked. Had she fallen asleep? She took a deep breath as she walked into the bathroom. She was going to have to ask Hobbs where he had gotten the gin. It must have come from a bad batch. Kay clenched her teeth. Her entire supply should be replaced. She had no intention of tolerating inferior products.

Staggering now, she poured soap into the tub as it filled with water. Suddenly a blazing flash of light exploded in her head and her eyes grew large in horror. Multi-colored little snakes swam around in her bath water. Horrible, slimy little creatures that were climbing the sides toward her.

She screamed over and over again, desperately trying to hang on to something, anything, as the room began spinning. It went faster and faster, and the snakes turned into horrible, giant green birds that pecked at her naked body. Then the room tilted and she was thrown into a deep, dark hole where she fell forever. There was no bottom and all the way down she screamed, her cries echoing in her ears and drying her mouth.

When she awoke, she was in a land of peace, resting on a soft bed of flowers. Kay opened her eyes to look directly into Derek's worried face.

"Hello, sweetheart," she said, reaching to put her arms around his neck.

"Kay, honey, are you all right?"

"I don't know." She laughed. "You tell me." She pulled to bring his head down, and was quite irritated when he resisted.

"I think you should rest, Kay." It was someone else speaking, and she turned in bewilderment.

"Dr. Bradford?"

"You had hallucinations," the doctor said.

The monsters peered around the edges of her mind. Hallucinations? "I must have fallen asleep," she said. "And had a nightmare. Derek, have Hobbs replace the gin. All I had was one drink."

Derek nodded, but was looking at the

doctor. "How long should she stay in bed?"

"How much can you take?" Kay asked, laughing.

Derek and the doctor looked at each other, and neither laughed. Dr. Bradford shrugged. "It could just have been something she ate."

"What'll it be, Mr. Prentiss?" the bartender asked.

"Scotch and soda, straight up, George."

Lucas slipped onto the barstool, letting his shoulders slump tiredly as he leaned his elbows on the bar. The drink appeared before him.

"Scotch and soda, straight up, Mr. Prentiss."

"Looks like you're a big man in this town," a voice said next to him.

Lucas was about to taste his drink, but the voice caused him to turn, a frown building on his face. It was that man who'd come with Leslie. What was his name?

"Jonas, Mr. Prentiss," the man said, as if in answer to his unspoken question. "Jonas Markham."

"Yes, of course. I remember." Lucas took a healthy pull on his drink, then swirled it around in his glass, staring at it for a long moment. He looked up suddenly. "I'm not really an important man in this town, Mr. Markham. You have me confused with my brother Lance."

"You're important enough," Jonas said.

"Oh?" Lucas glowered at the man, suspecting mockery.

"I've been a bartender for years," Jonas said. "And now I own a bar."

Turning back to face forward, Lucas had some more of his drink.

"Now, a bartender, he only knows two kinds of people by name," Jonas went on. "His heavy customers and important people. His heavy customers he calls by their first name and he remembers what they drink. Important people he calls by their surname and he always double-checks what they want. Doesn't want to take a chance of irritating them."

"Interesting observation," Lucas said.

"Your average bartender is a professional student of the human animal."

Lucas did not reply.

"Every day he's got people coming in. They belly up to the bar, drop their drawers—psychologically speaking—and dump on him, again psychologically speaking, of course."

"How did you meet Leslie?" Lucas asked. He was interested only in the man's relationship to Leslie, not his psychological observations.

"She collapsed outside the bar, cold and hungry, so we took care of her. Now she plays the piano and sings for our customers."

Leslie singing in a bar? "She's a classical pianist," Lucas said, unable to keep a note of horror from his voice. "She's had concert tours in all the major cities of Europe and America."

Jonas shrugged. "That didn't seem to harm her any. She's still got a nice touch."

"George," Lucas called, holding up his empty glass. He took a deep breath as he waited and stared in the mirror before him. Jonas seemed to be playing with his glass, rather than drinking. Lucas didn't like the man. What did he come in here for, if not to drink? "Thank you, George," Lucas said, then drank about a third of his glass. He let the liquor spread its warmth and relaxation throughout his being, but he still didn't like Jonas. Nothing was going to change that.

"Leslie was sick when she came to you," Lucas said. "She was suffering from a bad case of nerves and probably amnesia."

"I didn't have anything to do with that," Jonas said.

Lucas felt the muscles twitch in his jaw. "She's better now."

"I had a lot to do with that," he said.

Lucas saw the crooked smile come on the man's face in the mirror. He wanted to throw his glass at the image and smash it to pieces. Instead he swallowed his anger.

"We appreciate that," Lucas said. "And you have our thanks. Mine, my family's, and Leslie's family. And if there is anything we can do for you, we'd be more than happy—"

"I already have what I want."

The face in the mirror had a very definite smirk to it. Lucas rubbed his eyes with his thumb and forefinger to ease the pressure behind them. "Leslie is my wife," he said. "I have a marriage certificate to prove it."

"Leslie seems to have forgotten about that."

Lucas spun around and grabbed the man by the shoulder. "Look—"

"I'll give you a choice, fella," Jonas said quietly. "You can take your hands off me or you can eat your Wheaties through your nose the rest of your life."

The rage that burned within Lucas was quickly extinguished by the stares of several pairs of eyes. Lucas let his hand slip off. "Look, Mr. Markham," he said.

"Leslie is okay now. You've helped her, but she doesn't need you anymore. You can leave."

"You want me to walk out of her life?" Jonas asked.

"You're not a part of her life." Lucas looked quickly around, then back down at the bar. People were watching him. His voice had been rising; he'd have to control it.

"She hasn't moved back into your house, has she?" Jonas asked.

Lucas shook his head.

"Then I don't think Leslie considers you a part of her life," Jonas pointed out.

"I'm her husband," Lucas said. "Once she gets home and relaxes, she'll be fine."

"I don't see her knocking down any doors to get to your house."

"Damn it, man. She married me."

"Maybe that's what brought on her nervous breakdown."

"I am sick and tired of your insults." People were staring again, but Lucas didn't care anymore.

"Is there any problem here, Mr. Prentiss?"

"Relax, George," Jonas said. "I'm leaving."

Jonas put money down for his drink, then threw down some extra. "Give Mr.

Prentiss here another round, George. On me. Life hasn't been treating him too well lately."

George looked at the money, at Lucas's still half-full glass, and then slowly walked away. Lucas slumped back onto the stool. Damn that man. Leslie was coming back home with him where she belonged. He would talk to her and everything would be straightened out.

Stuart forced a pleasant smile on his face and circulated among the other attendees. Actually, the smile shouldn't have to be forced, he told himself. These civic dinners, much as he found them tiresome, were a way to delay going home to Jill.

Time had not improved their relationship, nor was it likely to. She was a bitch, a wicked, evil woman, and he rued the day he had met her.

"Stuart Brooks?"

Stuart looked up at the white-haired man before him, his hand extended. "Yes," Stuart said, shifting his drink to his other hand so he could shake the man's hand, even though his stomach was twisting in annoyance. Couldn't he have an evening out without being constantly reminded of Jill? Still, he could hardly blame this man. "Dr. Jamison, right?"

"Michael," he corrected with a smile. "Actually, I've been wanting to talk to you for some time now. Have you got a minute?"

"Sure, why not?" Stuart said with a sigh. They had about that much time before they were supposed to find their places at the tables. "Is it about Jill?"

For a moment, Dr. Jamison looked puzzled. "Jill?"

"My wife," Stuart explained. Maybe the man hadn't realized Jill had married him. "She's a patient of yours. Jill Foster Brooks."

The man burst into smiles. "Why, I had no idea you'd gotten married. Congratulations."

Sympathies were more appropriate, but Stuart wasn't one to air his dirty laundry in public. Though Dr. Jamison was certainly privy to it.

Dr. Jamison went on with a chuckle. "She was in not too long ago for a checkup and never said a word about getting married. You must have swept her off her feet."

Stuart tried to smile, but thought it would be safer to get off the subject of his marriage. "You said you wanted to talk to me. Was it about Jill?"

The doctor shook his head, a confused frown replacing the smile. "No, not at all.

She's a fine, healthy young woman. Why should you think there was a problem?"

Stuart just shrugged. "Well, in her condition—"

"In her condition?" The doctor was clearly puzzled, then his face brightened. "Oh, do you mean you're hoping to start a family? Well, that shouldn't be a problem. She should have no trouble getting pregnant."

There was a long pause during which Stuart's heart stopped. No trouble getting pregnant? But she *was* pregnant. Or was she? His hand tightened around his glass as he tried to ask the question in his mind without revealing the suspicions in his heart. "Are you sure we're talking about the same Jill Foster?" he asked carefully.

"How many are there?" the doctor asked with a laugh. "Tall, red hair, a rather aggressive lady who favors bright colors."

It was she, but there were other things Stuart still had to be sure of. He spoke slowly, though a terrible rage was building inside him. "Then, when she came to you for her checkup last month she wasn't pregnant?"

Dr. Jamison frowned at Stuart. "No, she hasn't been pregnant since I've been seeing her. Why?"

Why? Because he was just realizing that

he'd been every kind of a fool, that he'd let a scheming, conniving woman ruin his life. Stuart pasted a smile on his lips, hiding, he hoped, the murderous hatred he was feeling. "Well, we've been hoping . . ." He let his words drift away into implication.

The doctor's confusion was replaced with sympathy. "Well, keep trying," he said. "Now, let me buy you a drink and get to the real reason I approached you. I want to know if we can count on the newspaper's support of the hospital's new fund-raising drive."

The rest of the evening passed in a blur for Stuart. His impulse had been to leave as soon as he'd learned the truth about Jill, but he forced himself to stay. He was a man who abhorred violence, but the knowledge of Jill's trickery could very well drive him to it. He had to think and calm down. When he finally got home, he found Jill polishing her nails in the sunroom. She looked up in surprise when he came in.

"My goodness," she said, looking at his suit and tie. "Aren't we formal tonight. You planning on sleeping in that?"

"You lied to me." His voice was a low, threatening growl. He thought her face paled somewhat, but she concentrated on her nails.

Soaps & Serials™ Fans!

★ Order the *Soaps & Serials*™ books you have missed in this series.

★ Collect other *Soaps & Serials*™ series from their very beginnings.

★ Give *Soaps & Serials*™ series as gifts to other fans.

...see other side for ordering information

You can now order previous titles of *Soaps & Serials*™ Books by Mail!

Just complete the order form, detach, and send together with your check or money order payable to:

Soaps & Serials™
120 Brighton Road, Box 5201
Clifton, NJ 07015-5201

━━━━━━━━━━━━━━━━━━━━━━━━━

Please circle the book #'s you wish to order:

(A) The Young and The Restless........	1	2	3	4	5	6	7	8	9	10
(B) Days of Our Lives....	1	2	3	4	5	6	7	8	9	10
(C) Guiding Light.......	1	2	3	4	5	6	7	8	9	10
(D) Another World......	1	2	3	4	5	6	7	8	9	10
(E) As The World Turns..	1	2	3	4	5	6	7	8	9	10
(F) Dallas™	1	2	3	4	5	6	7	8	9	10
(G) Knots Landing™.....	1	2	3	4	5	6	7	8	9	10

Each book is $2.50 ($3.50 in Canada).

Total number of books circled_____ × price above = $ _____

Sales tax (CT and NY residents only) $ _____

Shipping and Handling $ _____ .95

Total payment enclosed $ _____
(check or money orders only)

Name _____

Address _____ Apt# _____

City _____

State _____ Zip _____

Telephone (_____) _____
Area Code

YR 10

"Whatever are you talking about?" She refused to look up at him.

"You conniving, miserable excuse for your mother's daughter. You lied to me."

"It's a little late in the day for games," Jill said, getting up. "Don't bother me until you're coherent."

He pushed her back into the chair, and suddenly his whole body began to shake. Good God, what had this witch done to him! He had never touched any woman in violence in his entire life. He stepped back behind a chair.

"You're not pregnant," he said.

"If you wanted to be a doctor, Stuart, you should have done something about it when you first went to college. I think it's a little late now."

"You are not pregnant."

"If you insist," Jill said, in a higher tone than usual. "I can make an appointment with my doctor and we can—"

"I met your doctor," Stuart said. "We had a long and very informative talk this evening." Her face turned ashen, but he got no satisfaction from it.

She leaned back slowly. "Well, you would have figured it out sooner or later." She sounded remarkably calm, considering her little game was through.

"Why?" he asked. "Why all this scheming and conniving?"

Jill put her feet up on the sofa and stared down at her nails. "Oh, come now," she said with a laugh in her voice.

"The only thing you arouse in me is loathing," he said. "Just tell me why, and without the coy behavior."

"Stuart, you can't be so dense."

"Damn it, Jill," he shouted. "If you wanted money I would have given it to you. After all, you are the daughter of the woman I love."

Her face turned hard and twisted. "Sure." She sneered. "All I had to do is fall to my knees and plead. And the big, generous man would throw some pennies at me."

"I wouldn't do that," he protested. "I've always been quite generous with family."

"I wanted it all, Stuart. Money, this house, position."

"Are you happy?" he asked.

"Very. I have it all."

"You don't have me."

Jill laughed, and the sound was not pleasant. "Oh, yes, I do, Mr. Stuart Brooks. As you and your cronies would so quaintly put it, I have you right by the short hairs."

Stuart put his hands behind him, clenching his fists hard. "I'll pay you," he said. "I'll give you everything, the house and every cent. I just want a divorce."

Jill shook her head. "No way, Jose. No way."

"We have nothing between us."

"I've got everything I want," Jill said. "And I'm not giving it up."

How could she be so cold and unfeeling? This was no sort of life for either of them, money or no money. His hands wanted to spring out and strangle her, so he intertwined them tightly as he started to walk out.

"Oh, Stuart," Jill called.

He stopped but did not turn around.

"You've already paid for it," she said easily. "I'm leaving my bedroom door open, just in case your appetites should return."

Stuart left, slamming the door in his anger, but her laughter followed him into the night.

Chapter Six

Dark Clouds

"Ladies, I'd like to see you in my chambers, please," the gray-haired judge told Leslie and Laurie as he stepped down from the bench. "The principals only," he said to the lawyers. "Counsel for both will wait out here."

He preceded Laurie and Leslie into his private office. "Close the door and sit down, please," he ordered without turning around. He opened his judicial robe and sat down, loosening his tie as he stared at the two women for a moment. Sighing, he reached for a thick folder.

"I am not looking forward to bringing this case to court," he told them. "So, my first objective will be to see if we can reach agreement here among ourselves."

He looked from one to the other as they each nodded in turn. Their father, Stuart Brooks, had been his friend for years, attending the same civic luncheons and serving on many of the same boards. He'd also known their mother, God bless her soul. It was a good thing she was no longer with them. This would have torn her apart.

"Have you ladies spoken to your father about this?" the judge asked.

"No," Laurie said quietly.

The judge ran his fingers through his bushy white mane, staring at the far wall. It seemed just a short time ago that these two were children and he'd given them candy from his jar of peppermints. Those first few years after he'd been appointed to the bench, Stuart used to bring his daughters around. They'd been such a happy family. At least it seemed so at the time.

"Don't you think there would be some merit to meeting with him?" the judge pushed. "Maybe this issue could be resolved within the family."

"No." The women spoke as one voice.

His spirits sagged along with his shoulders; he felt very old. Old and useless. No matter what he tried to do, this case was going to trial. He felt it in the air. He read it in the two firmly set faces before him.

"Our father has his own interests at the moment," Laurie said. Leslie nodded her agreement.

Yes, the judge remembered, his friend's marriage to Jill Foster, a contemporary of his daughters'. He didn't understand that at all, but then, he hadn't seen Stuart lately in their usual haunts, either. Maybe the man had changed. Certainly he did have his own interests at the moment.

The judge felt bound to act in a fatherly role, given the circumstances. "Do you two realize that, given the social position of your family, this trial will be a hot news item all over this state?"

Neither responded.

"Reporters will camp here," the judge said, his voice rising. "They will dig up every tidbit about every member of your family. They will not concern themselves with relevance to the case at hand."

Both women were staring down at the floor. Neither was willing to budge. They would not look at him or at each other.

"So be it," he said with a deep sigh, and opened the file on his desk. "Let's review what facts we have. The subject at issue is Brooks Prentiss." He glanced up quickly, but both women were still concentrating on the pattern of his rug. "The subject was born of Leslie Brooks Prentiss, and the father of record is one Lucas Prentiss."

The rug blurred and swirled together into a mélange of color. Leslie bit the inside of her lower lip and swallowed hard. The father of record. That's exactly what he was. Poor Lucas. That's all he'd ever be, a man of record. He'd lived in Lance's public shadow all his life and he couldn't escape it even in the privacy of his own family.

"Is that correct?"

Would Brooks ever know the identity of his biological father? Should he? What purpose would it serve? The family genes were the same.

"Leslie?"

Her head snapped up. "Yes, sir," she stammered.

"Are these facts, as I reviewed them so far, correct?"

Leslie hesitated. It was so stuffy in the office. She found breathing difficult.

"Leslie." Then he spoke to both of them. "Please excuse me for using your first names. Your married names and your maiden names are the same; your first names are the only things different. I am not trying to be familiar, although I have known you and your families for years," he finished wearily. "Now, Leslie, would you please confirm the facts I have just reviewed or tell me where they should be corrected?"

"Yes," Leslie said slowly. "Yes, I gave birth to Brooks."

"All right," the judge said, returning his attention to the file in front of him.

From the corner of her eye Leslie could see Laurie staring hard at her. Leslie shifted her gaze back to the floor.

Make her answer all of your question, Laurie cried in her heart. *Make her answer all of it;* but the old judge went on. Laurie's jaw tightened. Leslie had always looked so delicate and fragile that people were always giving her a pass. It hadn't mattered when all they were squabbling over were a few cookies, but now—

"The subject was then brought to the home of Lance and Laurie Prentiss. He was left there. Subsequently, Leslie Prentiss left her husband, Lucas Prentiss." He looked from one to the other.

"That's correct, judge," Laurie said, still looking at her downcast sister. "My sister, Leslie, gave me the child."

Leslie's head snapped up. "No, that's not what I meant to do. I only left Brooks with her temporarily."

"You gave him to me," Laurie shouted.

"No," Leslie screamed back.

"Ladies," the judge snapped, slamming his hand on the desk. "That's enough."

Laurie took a deep breath. She knew that she had to calm down. Leslie had always had things her way because she acted so sweet and innocent. People would attack Laurie, telling her to quit bullying her sweet sister.

"She came to me, judge." Laurie was almost pleading. "She said that she wouldn't be able to care for Brooks. She asked me to raise him."

"I was sick. I was confused," Leslie said.

"How do you know you're well now?" Laurie asked.

Her sister turned tortured eyes toward her. "That's cruel, Laurie."

Laurie just wanted to run away. She was a battlefield of conflicting emotions. Love for Brooks. Love for Leslie. Sibling rivalry. Fear of losing Brooks. She just wanted to hide, but her love for Brooks won out. It wouldn't let her do anything less than fight.

"Brooks came from my body," Leslie said.

"I gave him my heart," Laurie responded.

The judge looked at them both, and their pain tore at his heart. He had come to his judgeship so full of caring and enthusiasm. Then, slowly, the venality of his friends and neighbors wore at his humanity. Now their children were coming to him, with the same kinds of problems. He'd had no effect on the world. Not even on the small piece of it that he occupied. He was a useless old man.

"Trial proceedings will begin a week from Friday," he said tiredly. "In my court-room at ten A.M. Please return to your respective counsel."

They stood up and without a word left his chambers.

He stared at the door long and hard. Twenty-five years on the bench, and it had all been for naught.

"The doctor said you're supposed to rest," Derek protested.

Kay frowned and patted the bed next to her. "Don't be such an old fuddy-duddy," she complained. "I'm feeling fine."

"You didn't seem fine yesterday."

"That was yesterday. Come on, I'm lonesome in this big old bed by myself."

She wasn't the invalid type, and all this fussing over her was getting annoying. There was nothing wrong with her; she felt great. That episode yesterday had been frightening, that was true, but she was managing to push it somewhat back from her consciousness. However, with a little cooperation from Derek, she'd be too pleasantly occupied to give it another thought.

"Let me show you just how well I feel," she teased.

"No, you're going to lie back and rest." Derek pushed her back gently and pulled the covers over her.

Kay just lay there, pouting up at him. "Pretty please," she said.

"I'm not playing around," Derek scolded and walked over to pull the drapes shut.

Fine. If he wasn't going to keep her company, she'd have to settle for something else to keep her happy. She surely wasn't about to go politely to sleep like a little kid. "Where are my chocolates?" she asked.

"They're in your sitting room. I told Hobbs to throw them out the next time he's up here."

"For heaven's sake," she exclaimed. "Why?"

"Who knows what caused your problem?"

"I told you what did it," she said, sitting up. Why were they all making such a big deal out of this? "It was no big mystery. I had a bad drink on an empty stomach and I was tired from too little sleep."

Derek shook his head. "I don't know. The way Hobbs tells it, you were in bad shape."

"Derek! You are taking the word of a

man who thinks nuns are wild women. It was a quick thing and it passed. It's no big deal. I feel much better."

He pulled the other drape shut without replying.

"Can I get up?"

"Nope."

"Then give me back my chocolates."

"Nope."

"I won't rest."

"Yes, you will."

"But Derek," she wailed. "Suzanne gave those chocolates to me. They're a token of peace from your ex-wife. Now, how can I refuse to eat them?"

"The fact that she gave you a box of expensive chocolates has nothing to do with it."

Kay smiled like a little girl. "Can I have just one piece?"

Derek sighed and went into the next room. He was back in a few moments with the box. "Here," he said. "But only one."

She selected a piece and, ignoring his frown, took a second one. Derek just shook his head, then went to shut the last drape. He picked up the box as he walked by the bed.

"Can I have a drink of water, Daddy?" Kay giggled.

Derek just bent over and gave her a kiss. "I want you better," he said softly.

"You are not a woman meant to be in bed alone."

"So join me," she invited. "I promise I'll rest much better if you're here."

He just shook his head and straightened up. "We'll see how you are tomorrow."

He left the room, carrying the box of chocolates down to the kitchen with him. Why in the world did Suzanne buy Kay candy? he wondered. Well, obviously, to get on Kay's good side, but why should Suzanne want that? He couldn't figure it out but, wanting nothing that came from Suzanne in the house, he tossed the box in the garbage. Suzanne had been nothing but trouble back when he'd been married to her, and he had no reason to think she'd changed.

"Don't make anything elaborate for dinner," he told the cook on his way out. "If we're hungry, we'll have you broil some hamburgers."

"Very good, sir."

Feeling rather lost without Kay, Derek wandered out on the patio. The sun was warm and there was a gentle breeze to add to the perfection of the afternoon, but he felt little of it. Kay insisted that she felt fine now, but the whole situation troubled him. Certainly he hadn't known Kay for very long, but Hobbs had, and the old man insisted that nothing like this had ever happened to her before, not even years back when she'd had a drinking problem.

Derek sighed and frowned at the pots of gardenias bordering the patio, breathing in the sweet fragrances and wishing they could soothe his troubled soul. He cared about Kay deeply and couldn't bear for anything to happen to her.

From Hobbs's description of yesterday's incident, how could she be fine today? Derek had arrived at the end of the attack, but the old butler had related the incident to him in horrible detail. This was not a case of the twenty-four-hour flu.

The patio was too quiet for his restless thoughts, and he got to his feet, wandering down a path through the garden. The flowers and shrubbery didn't interest him in the slightest, but the movement of his feet kept his thoughts from overcoming him. Nothing could happen to Kay. He couldn't stand it if it did.

"Sir, sir, come quickly, please."

Derek spun around to see Hobbs hurrying across the garden toward him. "Please, sir," Hobbs called out. "It's the madam. Something's wrong again."

Derek broke into a run, reaching the house well before the aging butler. The house suddenly seemed too huge; he seemed to be moving through it in slow motion. The stairs had doubled in length, but finally he reached the top. A terrified maid, tears streaming down her cheeks, waited at the door to Kay's bedroom. He burst into it to find Kay trying to rip a pillow apart like some dog.

"Kay!"

She turned wild eyes toward him and growled.

"Oh, my God." It was worse than he'd pictured from Hobbs's description of yesterday's attack. He moved forward cautiously. "Kay. It's me, Derek."

Suddenly she threw herself at him, her face contorted in rage, but her body fell short and she dissolved in a heap at his feet, twitching uncontrollably. Strange, animallike sounds came from her mouth.

"Kay, poor Kay," he muttered as he pulled her into his arms, trying to rock her gently as one might a terrified child. But it had little effect on her.

She seemed totally unaware of his identity, unaware of his presence. Her jaws were locked tight; her eyes appeared to have rolled back into her head. Derek was terrified, afraid of what was happening to her and what she might do to him, but he didn't let go of her. His love was stronger than his fear.

"Hobbs," he screamed over his shoulder. "Call the doctor."

"He's on his way."

"Call an ambulance."

Hobbs left quickly, and for long, endless minutes, Derek held Kay tightly to him. She would rest quietly for a while, then suddenly burst into frantic movement, trying to free herself from his restraint, only to subside abruptly again. Lord, what was happening to her?

The siren sounded in the distance, a bleak token of his despair that grew louder along with his fears. It seemed hours before it actually got to the house. Then he heard the doctor's voice in the hall and quick steps on the marble floor racing toward the stairs. He relaxed his arms; help was at hand.

Kay was quiet, but not aware, as he thought, for the moment his arms relaxed she turned into a wild animal again. She hissed and growled, twisted from his arms with a strength much greater than his. Her eyes flickering with a maniacal fire, she scratched and clawed at him. He tried to recapture her arms, but it was hopeless; she was a tiger unwilling to be caged again. Sitting on the floor as he had been, he was her helpless victim, unable to flee. She scratched his cheek with her nails, spat and hissed her rage as she circled him slowly, the tiger about to pounce.

"Kay!" he cried. "It's me. It's Derek. Kay, can you hear me?" He kept trying to get his arms around her again, but she was too quick for him.

Then the doctor was there along with the ambulance attendants. As Derek watched in growing horror, they wrestled her to the floor and into a straitjacket. There she lay, his beloved wife, writhing and twisting on the floor. The moans and cries had turned to curses as she damned everyone present, plus people he'd never heard of, to hell. Her lovely face was contorted with hatred and rage.

Derek couldn't bear to watch, but couldn't turn away either. He wanted to comfort her somehow, to tell her how he loved her and beg her to come back to him. But he sat frozen on the floor, unable to move or speak to her.

Once she was subdued in the straitjacket, the doctor prepared a syringe. "A sedative," he told Derek.

Again the attendants held her still while the doctor gave her the injection. Then slowly, almost imperceptibly, she relaxed. The rage left her face, her limbs sagged. Her body slumped into unconsciousness. Only then did Derek realize he'd been holding his breath.

He got to his feet as they put Kay into her bed, then silently followed the doctor into her sitting room next door. Her heavy, labored breathing seemed to echo around them.

"We're going to have to commit her," the doctor said slowly. "Next time she may hurt herself or someone else more than just the scratches you got. We need to watch her more carefully."

Derek just nodded slowly. His world, which had been so perfect, was suddenly falling apart.

"Would you like me to look at that cheek?" the doctor asked.

Derek shook his head. What were a few scratches compared to Kay's problem? "What in the world is the matter with Kay?"

The doctor shrugged. "I was hoping you'd be able to help me." He sat down slowly. "Has there been a substantial change in her behavior in recent weeks?"

"Just today and yesterday," Derek said. "We called you both times."

"Has she been drinking heavily? You know she had a drinking problem some years back."

"No." Derek shook his head. "She doesn't need the alcohol anymore. She just has occasional drinks. Nothing she can't handle."

The doctor put his fingertips together

and stared at them. The silence stretched into centuries, and with it, Derek's fears grew.

"I don't know how to phrase this judiciously," the doctor said carefully. "But has Kay been taking drugs? Especially any hallucinogenics."

Derek was floored. "You mean the stuff that burns your brain?"

The doctor nodded.

"No way," Derek said, shaking his head positively. "I don't think that's something you can hide. No, she's been real happy lately. She's even handling my ex-wife in a reasonably pleasant manner."

"Well, I certainly don't have any other ideas." The doctor stood up, reaching for his bag. "We'll just have to keep her confined while we run some tests."

"Thanks, doctor," Derek said. He got up wearily and shook the doctor's hand. "I just don't understand what's going on."

"Life is full of mysteries. I only hope this is one we can solve," the doctor replied. "I'll have the ambulance transport her to the sanitarium."

Leslie's arms were starting to hurt from carrying the packages, so she decided to rest a moment. She sat down on a park bench and rubbed first one shoulder, then the other. It was a pleasant little park, Leslie thought, leaning back to rest.

She had gone out that morning to buy some gifts for Brooks. It was going to be a wonderful morning, she told herself, envisioning all the darling little outfits she'd buy him, all the cuddly stuffed animals. Maybe she'd even look at furniture and plan his room. Laurie had made a nice nursery, Leslie had to admit, but she would make a better one. After all, she was Brooks's mother, and a mother knew how to do these things better.

But the morning didn't go as she planned. The little suits and sleepers were there to be bought, but she didn't know what size. Oh, she knew how old he was when the salesgirls asked, but when they brought out sleepers they thought would fit, Leslie thought they looked too big, or too small. The salesgirls would smile condescendingly then as if she were the baby's distant aunt or merely a friend of the mother.

I'm his mother, Leslie had wanted to scream over and over again, but didn't, knowing that their smiles would have turned cold then. A distant relative was allowed not to know a size; a mother wasn't. Leslie had fled the infant clothing department and took refuge in toys.

But things went no better there. Every animal she loved seemed to look familiar. Was it the same one Laurie had bought for Brooks? If so, then Leslie didn't want it. She finally settled on a few things that the salesclerk assured her were brand-new, but the whole experience had worn her out. Now, rather than take her gifts over to Laurie's home, she was sitting here in the park trying to gather her strength and her courage.

Sounds of children at play drifted up to her. Leslie turned around and saw a little playground. It was filled with swings, sandboxes, tunnels, and all sorts of things for toddlers to creep and crawl over. The children there now were having a wonderful time. Their laughter brought a smile to Leslie's lips.

How Brooks would love playing here when he was a little older, she thought. She could almost see his happy little face as he sped down the low slide, or hear his laughter and delight as he swung high in the little swings. The sand castles he would build in the sandbox would be magnificent, and when he was done he would come running to her for a hug.

Leslie stopped, a frown closing off her daydreams. What was she thinking of? This park was close to Laurie's home, not her own. When Brooks was old enough to play here, he would be living with her, not Laurie. She tried to think of a park near her home, but drew a blank. There was one, she thought, but she had never seen a wonderful little play area in it. Well, no matter. Brooks didn't need a swing to make him happy; he'd be happy just being with her. With his mother.

Leslie turned, ready to gather her packages together, when she stopped. Laurie, pushing Brooks in a stroller, had rounded a clump of trees and was heading for the playground. The little boy was laughing. Leslie could see that, even at her distance. For some reason, it hurt. She knew Laurie had taken good care of him, but somehow, Leslie had never thought that Brooks would love her in return. Laurie wasn't his mother, but how was a baby supposed to know that?

Leslie frowned with uneasy feelings nagging at her. She slid over to one side of the bench, which was partially blocked from the play area by bushes. She didn't want Laurie to see her.

Brooks was too small to play on the equipment, so Laurie brought the stroller over to a bench where she joined the other mothers. One was a grandmotherly sort who began to fuss over Brooks immediately. *That's my little boy*, Leslie wanted to run over and tell them. *Isn't he the sweetest thing you ever saw?* The woman must have asked to hold him, for Laurie lifted Brooks from the stroller and gave him to her.

Brooks was content for only a moment, then began to cry. *He wants his mother,* Leslie told herself. She was on her feet without thinking, ready to rush over and comfort him. *He needs his mother,* she thought.

But before her feet could even start moving, Laurie had reached for him. His tiny arms reached out for her in turn, his little face still teary but filled with obvious longing. Leslie's heart stood still, wrenched with terrible pain.

As soon as Brooks was back in Laurie's arms, his tears stopped and his laughter started again, but one dimpled hand clutched her shirt as if he would never let go. Leslie sank back onto the bench, her eyes closed as she fought back her own tears. Brooks thought he had his mother.

Unable to watch any longer, Leslie swept her packages up into her arms and hurried from the park. She had thought coming home to Genoa City would solve all her problems, that the answers she would find would be nothing but happy ones.

But that hadn't happened. There was Jonas, still worrying over her. There was Lucas, who obviously loved her, while her feelings toward him were merely warm. There was Laurie, who feared and almost hated her. And then there was Brooks.

Leslie's arms ached to hold her son, her heart wept with missing him, but he didn't know her at all. His eyes didn't light up with love when she came near.

What had she accomplished by coming back? What had she done but promise pain to Lucas, Jonas, and Laurie? And to the one she loved best, little Brooks?

Chapter Seven

Lost Loves

"To us," Lucas toasted once the waiter had poured the champagne and left them alone in the secluded corner of the restaurant.

Leslie tried to smile, if not share in his toast, but the seriousness in his face, that little boy's earnestness beaming from his blue eyes, weighed her down. Everything about her felt heavy and sluggish: her breathing, her heart, and especially her arm, the arm that was supposed to raise her glass in support of Lucas's toast. That arm didn't want to move at all. Was there an "us" to toast to?

Lucas set his own glass slowly on the table. Tired lines spread from his eyes and filled his face; the earnestness in his eyes had turned to pain. Leslie looked down at her glass. She wasn't hungry anymore; she just wanted to run away to a place where she wouldn't hurt anybody ever again. To a place where no one had such high expectations of her, but would let her be herself.

"I'm sorry, Lucas," she said at last. "I just don't have a taste for wine tonight. I guess I should have said something before you ordered."

"We can toast with our water glasses," he suggested.

"I'm just so tired tonight." She didn't respond to his suggestion, yet she really wasn't ignoring him. She'd just put him on hold, where she'd always had him. He deserved better.

"Do you want to go home?" he asked.

Home? Where was home? Her father's house where she grew up? That wasn't her home anymore, not since Jill had moved in. That little apartment above Jonas's place? No, that had been a way station, a place of refuge when she needed it. She didn't need it anymore. Lucas's house? That had never been her home. It was just a house filled with guilt, which squeezed and oppressed her whenever she came near.

"Leslie," Lucas said quietly, taking her hand. "We don't have to eat if you're not hungry. We can go home, and if you're hungry later, I can fix you something."

That was where she wanted to go.

Home. Back to her own home here in Genoa City. Back to the little apartment where her piano lived. That safe, quiet refuge that was hers alone. But what she wanted was her piano and the solace of music, not to spend a quiet evening there with Lucas. She looked into his eyes. She had to tell him that, but how?

"Leslie, are you all right?"

She forced a smile to her lips. She owed him something, this husband of hers who'd been so patient and kind. She owed him at least an evening together, for him to try to win her back. He wouldn't, but she owed him the chance to try.

"I don't want any wine," she said. "But I do want to eat."

He looked a long while at her, as if trying to read her heart, then nodded his head. At his signal, a waiter brought them menus. The heaviness returned again as Leslie gazed at the long list of entrees. She'd told Lucas she was hungry, but which of these things could she force down her throat?

"Everything sounds so delicious," Leslie said. "It's hard to pick one."

"Let me suggest the broiled swordfish, madam." Someone had stopped at the table.

She lowered the menu to find a man smiling down at her. "Jonas!" Leslie exclaimed. A good part of the weight dragging her down drifted away. Jonas was a refuge. He didn't demand anything of her. "How nice to see you."

Lucas ignored him, studying his menu.

Leslie smiled her own welcome at Jonas, determined not to let him escape. "Would you believe in all my world travels I've never had swordfish?"

"Now is your chance to be wild," Jonas said. "Right here in your old home town. Genoa City, U.S.A."

Leslie laughed. It was so nice to relax in the comfort of his easy attitude. "Okay. They say you only live once."

"That's the way I understand it to work."

He stood in silence while Leslie reviewed the menu one more time. "I will accept your suggestion," she announced as she closed her menu with a flair.

"You won't be disappointed," Jonas said.

"Have you had the swordfish this evening?" Leslie asked as she laid her menu next to her plate.

"No," he replied. "Last night. I haven't eaten yet."

"Well, then please join us." The words had barely cleared her lips and already Leslie desperately wished she could pull them back. The tired lines on Lucas's face were replaced by a dark mask of hate. If looks could kill, Jonas would be dead and buried in a matter of seconds.

But he seemed not to notice Lucas's evident displeasure. Or else he didn't care. "That's very kind of you. Don't mind if I do." He wrapped his face in a smile, pulled up a chair, and signaled for the waiter, carefully avoiding Lucas's gaze.

"It's so nice to have company," Leslie said. She covered Lucas's hand with her own, hoping to draw him out of his dark mood. Lucas might not want Jonas here, but she certainly did. She couldn't take much more of Lucas's possessiveness and his reminders of a love that they supposedly shared, but which awoke no memories in her.

"I was satisfied with just your company," Lucas pointed out.

"Obviously Leslie wasn't satisfied with yours," Jonas mocked.

"Gentlemen, please," she cried. "I just wanted to share the evening with two people who are special to me. Is that so terrible?"

Suddenly Leslie felt as if she were back in high school and two studs were courting her favor. Why had she thought Jonas was a refuge? He wasn't. He was a man, with a man's needs. Jonas was in love with her and he wanted to win out over

Lucas, just as Lucas hoped to eliminate Jonas from the picture.

Leslie's hand slipped away from Lucas as she stared out over the dining room. There was no place of refuge for her anymore, not with her memory coming back stronger every day. Everywhere she turned there were people wanting, needing, and demanding of her. How would she be able to handle little Brooks's demands on top of everything else? Leslie pushed that thought away as the waiter came to take their orders.

"I'll have the chicken Vesuvio," Jonas told the waiter.

"Not the swordfish? Is there something wrong with it?" Lucas mocked.

"I had it last night, if you remember me telling you," Jonas snapped back. "It was delicious, but I like a little variety."

Reluctantly Leslie returned to her two companions. "Lucas, Jonas. Please. You don't have to be friends, but please, for my sake, can't you be civil?"

The two men looked down at the table in front of them and pouted. If she weren't so tired, Leslie would have laughed aloud. Would she have to share her time equally with the two little boys?

But they weren't little boys. No matter how much she wanted them to be, no matter how much she wanted to laugh and make light of things, they were men. Both of them.

Jonas ordered an old-fashioned, and when the drink came he held out the cherry for her as he always did in his own nightclub. Leslie caught sight of Lucas's glare and looked away for a moment. Why did everything have to be so complicated?

When her gaze returned to her companions, Jonas was putting the cherry in the ashtray while Lucas gave him a sneer of triumph. Leslie's stomach juices turned sour; she felt the fire of their acid.

It seemed like ages before the food finally came and the smell almost gagged her, but Leslie ate because it gave her something to do. The trouble was, she didn't want either man, she realized. She wanted peace and quiet. She just wanted to run away and be alone. But where did that leave little Brooks?

Water. Water. Kay's mouth was so dry that her tongue was like a dry rag. Water. She was so thirsty.

Her eyes fluttered, then slowly opened. Light green walls surrounded her and clean white sheets cuddled her. She wasn't in a desert. Thank God, it was just a dream. But she was still thirsty. She sat up in bed and suddenly fear gripped her. Green walls and white sheets. No wallpaper. No pink sheets. This wasn't her room. She wanted to scream, but an icy claw gripped her vocal cords. She tried, but only air came out. No sound.

"Good morning, Mrs. Thurston."

Kay stared at the white-suited woman. Thurston? She was Kay Chancellor.

"How are you feeling?"

No, wait. She was married to Derek, Derek Thurston. She was Mrs. Thurston.

"Where am I?" Kay asked.

"You're at Willow Haven Sanitarium," the nurse replied. "Let me take your temperature, please." She took Kay's wrist and found the pulse.

Willow Haven? Kay felt a heaviness on her chest. Willow Haven was the place for nut cases. Rich nut cases, but nut cases nonetheless.

"Who put me in here?" Kay demanded when the thermometer was removed.

The nurse wrote some data on a form. "You're Dr. Bradford's patient," she replied.

Kay persisted in her questions. "But how did I get here?"

"An ambulance service brought you."

"Dr. Bradford put me in here?" Kay desperately searched and peered through the debris cluttering her mind. She'd always been a sharp person, and the blank spaces where the past few days should have been were very disconcerting.

A look of disapproval slipped past the nurse's professional mask. "I'd say you put yourself in here," she snapped.

"Why?"

The nurse straightened her mask and put it back in place. "You'll have to speak to Dr. Bradford," she said coolly.

"Call him," Kay ordered. "I want to see him."

"He'll be here this afternoon."

"Damn it," Kay shouted. "I want to see him now. So call him."

The woman turned on her heel and walked out. The door shut with a re-sounding click. A shiver ran through Kay as she realized that the door was locked. She was a prisoner here. But why?

Since she was still thirsty, Kay sat up, resisting the impulse to scream, and poured herself a second glass. Her thirst quenched for the moment, she swung her legs over the side of the bed and gingerly stood up.

Some of the blanks were filling in, but that wasn't any more comforting. She remembered the horrible nightmares. Monsters, snakes, and bugs crawling all over her body. The walls turning purple, black, and red. That certainly was not her usual decor. What in the world was going on?

A key rattled in the door, and Kay held her breath.

"You have a visitor," the nurse announced.

Derek came through the door and hesitated.

"Derek." Kay flew into his arms. He kissed her gently, as though she were a bruised flower, so she kissed him roughly, with the normal hunger they shared. She was still strong, still in need of him. They kissed again and again, speaking without words until she was sure he knew her soul. Then she just leaned on his chest while he held her. It felt so good. Good enough so that she had the strength to ask him a question.

"Why am I here?"

"You've been real sick, honey," he said. "You've been hallucinating."

"Hallucinating?"

She looked up into Derek's face, certain he was joking, but all she saw there was concern. No duplicity, no conniving. That wouldn't be Derek anyway.

"Yes. You were seeing weird things. Bugs. Snakes."

"Monsters," she added.

"Yeah." He nodded. "To tell you the truth, you scared the hell out of me. You

were acting like you were on acid, but I
know you don't do any drugs."

Kay shook her head. What in the world
was going on?

"But you know, you were right about
Suzanne," Derek said, breaking the silence.

"Suzanne?" Kay was starting to feel like
an idiot with her constant dumb questions.

Derek nodded. "She's turning out to be
real nice, just like you said."

She pushed away from him and walked
over to the other side of the room to sit
down. Kay put her hands to her head; she
was feeling faint. "I'm sorry I'm so slow,
Derek, but I'm having a hard time concentrating. What's this about Suzanne?"

"She's been calling to see how you are.
She's been real worried."

She's been calling? Why? Kay let her
hands fall to her lap and stared at Derek.
He returned his usual open, little-boy
look.

"She even took me out to dinner last
night so I wouldn't be alone," Derek said.
"That was really nice of her."

Kay's stare danced on the edge of be-
coming a glare, but she fought to keep the
blandness in her face. "That certainly
was."

"Our house is really nice," Derek went

on. "But when you're not there, it has all the hominess of a museum."

A warmth welled up inside Kay for a moment. Derek truly loved her and this was as hard on him as it was on her. Almost immediately, the warmth was replaced by anger. Why was this happening to them? She turned away to fight back her rage.

Derek was immediately by her side. "I'm sorry, honey. You've had a hard time these last few days, and you're probably tired."

He was blaming himself for having upset her, which wasn't true, but she couldn't explain to him. Not yet, not until she figured this whole thing out.

He gave her a tender kiss, then held her. "Don't worry, babe," he said, patting her shoulder. "Dr. Bradford will find the problem and then everything will be fine again."

Would it?

Derek kissed her again before straightening up. "I'll see you again tomorrow," Derek said. "Just relax and get your rest. Dr. Bradford said that might be all you need."

When the door clicked shut after him, Kay let go of the leash on her emotions. Anger started in her quivering stomach, traveling from there to lodge in her hands.

She folded them in her lap to stop the shaking.

Suzanne, Suzanne. That woman's name was starting to surface a great deal lately. Just about the time her own troubles started. Where was the connection? Was there a connection? There had to be, but Kay's head was starting to ache. There were too many blanks to be filled in, and she needed more strength before she could do it. She went to her bed and lay down. She would find the answers, she vowed. She would find the answers and make whoever was responsible pay.

Leslie breathed a sigh of relief once the cab pulled away from the curb, taking her away from the restaurant. The scene at dinner had been close to turning ugly. Lucas had wanted her to go home with him and Jonas wanted her to go back to their rooms in the hotel. She chose instead to go to her own apartment in Genoa City. It probably was the wisest choice, regardless of her own feelings, she thought with a smile. Now, at least, both men were equally aggravated with her, so a fight had been avoided.

Leaning against the seat back, she closed her eyes. Because of all her traveling, she tended to look upon Genoa City as home, a refuge from the pushing and shoving of an uncaring world. But now, things were getting so complex and so full of tension that she wanted to run. Leslie didn't care where as long as it was far away.

"Here you go, lady."

The cab had stopped and Leslie quickly sat up. The driver grunted, even though her tip was generous, and sped off into the night. Although she chastised herself for her paranoia, Leslie looked up and down the street. She wanted to be alone with neither Lucas nor Jonas around, and once she was satisfied no one had followed her here, she went into her apartment.

She hadn't been back here since her marriage to Lucas, short that it had been, and a musty smell greeted her entry. Normally when she traveled, Leslie had the furniture all covered, but she hadn't done it this time and a film of dust covered everything.

She took a dust cloth from the kitchen and went to work dusting her piano, then found the furniture polish and lovingly polished every surface, crack, and corner. Only after that was done did she sit down to the instrument.

Her fingers moved tentatively to the keys. They started slowly, she and her piano, like old friends who'd grown apart.

Each one feeling out the other. Testing a key here, a note there.

Then, easily and surely, without the feeling for or knowledge of crossing a boundary, they slipped into total acceptance. Her fingers danced, skipping lightly and gaily across the keys.

Leslie had played pop tunes at Jonas's nightclub, but this piano was an old friend. They had so much to catch up on. They moved into their favorite, a lively Chopin waltz.

When she finished the piece, tears were flowing down her cheeks. She was home, her real home. Nowhere else would she feel so welcome, so comfortable, and so relaxed.

Leslie kicked off her shoes and poured herself a glass of water. There wasn't anything else to drink, but it didn't matter. Even the water tasted better at home. Then she began playing again.

She played into the night. In her bare feet, Leslie felt as if she were sitting with an old friend from high school. Now that the initial uncertainty was over, they had so much to catch up on. They discussed old friends, friends that Leslie had made in traveling the world.

To conquer her fear of the large crowds that came to see her play, Leslie had taken each piano she played in concerts as a new friend. She'd seen each of them a number of times. The dark polish of the one on the stage in Bonn, the scar on the left leg of the piano in Paris, and who could ever forget how the lights brought out the red in the London instrument?

There was so much to talk about, and where the time went nobody knew. It was three o'clock when Leslie found herself on the couch. She didn't remember how she'd gotten there. It was so wonderful just to be playing, to be away from the cares and the irritations of people. Her music had none of that. Her music had peace and shared it unselfishly with her, soothing her sorrows and filling her soul with joy.

Leslie got up stiffly and went into the bedroom to lie down. Bach, Beethhoven, Chopin. They were all her family. She had been a fool to leave them. She never would again.

Chapter Eight

Loving Visits

"Good morning, Laurie," Leslie said quietly and uneasily as she stood outside Laurie's door. "I hope I didn't come over too early."

"No, we're up early," Laurie said. "Babies tend to be early risers." Laurie's words were friendly, but her tone was short, curt. Wariness and suspicion danced about in her eyes. Pleasantness had not yet arrived.

"May I come in?" Leslie asked.

Laurie hesitated a long moment, then stood aside. Leslie made her way to Laurie's living room while her sister quietly followed her.

"Why don't you make us some tea?" Leslie suggested.

Laurie didn't say anything, but she didn't hesitate, either. She turned and left the room as Leslie sat down. The room was neat with touches of elegance. Like Laurie herself, Leslie thought. A magnificent framed print of a sunrise caught her eye. Its bright colors brought hope and joy into the room. Leslie took a deep breath, willing her quivering nerves to be still. She turned and saw a picture of little Brooks on the mantel. Darling, precious little Brooks.

"I love you more than anything in the whole world," she whispered to the photograph, even as tears stung at her eyes.

She heard a noise and turned away, fighting to regain her control as Laurie returned. By the time she'd silently placed the two cups of tea and the plate of cookies on the low table between them, Leslie was able to smile her thanks, though Laurie's eyes seemed to flit everywhere but within Leslie's gaze. Leslie understood and reached for a cookie to break the spell.

"I spent last night in my apartment," Leslie said as she nibbled on it.

Laurie glanced at her for a moment.

"I played the piano a good part of the night." Leslie picked up her tea and took a few tentative sips. "It felt good."

"Music was always your life," Laurie said.

"Always has been and always will be."

They looked at each other then. Leslie

wasn't sure, but she thought she saw a thawing in the frost of Laurie's eyes. Maybe all that bickering of childhood was the fuel that forged their love.

"Would you like some more tea?" Laurie asked.

Leslie nodded and held her cup out. "I feel so much better now," she went on to say. "I'm literally itching to return to the concert tour."

"Have you talked to Lucas about it?"

Leslie stopped and put her cup down before walking over to the window. The sun was shining on the grass and trees in the parks that surrounded Laurie and Lance's home. What a wonderful, happy place for a child to grow up in! Leslie savored that moment of peace, refusing to let any of her own pain mar it.

"I've been lucky in a lot of ways," Leslie said, still staring out the window. "I've had good men in my life." She turned to face her sister. "First there was Dad. He'll always be tops on my list."

Laurie's face twisted in a frown. "I don't know what he sees in that woman," she said. "She's our age, for heaven's sake."

Leslie shrugged. "Don't the Indians have some kind of saying about not judging another until you walk a mile in their moccasins?"

Laurie just shook her head. "But still . . ."

Leslie pulled back the conversation before she lost her resolve. "Anyway, we were talking about the men in my life."

"Yes." Laurie laughed. "Who came after Dad?"

"High school was pretty bleak," Leslie admitted. "But, then I had Brad." She was silent a long moment as she moved along her list to Lance. The one love she wasn't allowed to mention or think of, not now that he belonged to Laurie. "Then I had Lucas, and Jonas found me when I really needed help."

"What's this have to do with anything?" Laurie asked, though her voice wasn't as suspicious as her words.

"The only constant I have had in my whole life is music." Leslie turned again to gaze out the window. "That is my one true love. That's what I'm going to return to."

"You haven't talked to Lucas about it."

Leslie didn't turn around. "I know that Lucas loves me, but so does Jonas."

A bird's song filled the silence and the world drifted.

"Who do you love?" Laurie asked quietly.

"I'm fond of them both."

Leslie turned around and returned to her seat. Laurie's wide eyes followed her.

"Fond," Leslie continued after having some more of her tea. "Maybe even very fond. Both came forward and helped me when I needed it."

"But?" Laurie prompted.

"But, no matter which I choose, I will hurt someone. And, no matter which I'd choose, I still wouldn't be happy."

"So you're not going to choose either."

"I'm going to choose my first love," Leslie said.

"You're really going back to the concert tour?" Laurie asked, as if she couldn't believe this was something Leslie had thought through. "All that practicing and all that traveling?"

Leslie nodded and Laurie looked away, down at the floor. Leslie saw her hand tremble ever so slightly.

"I realize it," Leslie said quietly.

Laurie looked up, a question in her eyes.

Leslie went on: "The concert circuit is no life for a child."

There was a long moment of pure silence, during which Leslie looked into Laurie's eyes and poured out her heart, told her sister of her loves and her fears and of her sacrifices. Of the gift she was giving Laurie of her son.

Laurie burst into tears and Leslie went to take her sister in her arms. A lump filled Leslie's throat, and she had to swallow several times before she was able to speak.

"I want you to keep little Brooks," Leslie said in a husky voice, putting into words what her eyes had already said. "I want you to raise him for both of us."

Laurie continued sobbing.

"I want you and Lance to give him the normal life that I never could."

Her sister pulled back, trying to control her tears. She pulled a tissue from her pocket and blew her nose, then took several slow, deep breaths.

"Thank you," Laurie said. Her lip began quivering, and she paused until it stopped. "Thank you for the most wonderful gift I've ever received in my whole life."

"And you'll let me see him whenever I'm in town?"

Laurie nodded. She was holding her lip in her teeth, obviously not trusting herself to speak.

"I can be his aunt, his very favorite aunt."

Laurie nodded again.

"I'll write him letters and send him gifts

from all over the world. Will you read him my letters, Laurie?" Leslie was able to ignore her own pain in light of Laurie's happiness.

Her sister smiled her agreement.

"And when I visit him, I'll tell him of all the wonderful places I've visited. Then, when he grows up, maybe he can be a diplomat, welcomed in all the courts of the world."

"Maybe he'll love music," Laurie said. "Like his mother."

"He's a Brooks, Laurie. Whatever he does, he'll do magnificently."

They hugged each other hard, very very hard. Leslie loved Laurie and she knew her sister loved her. They would always be there, for each other and for their loved ones.

When they parted, tears were again streaming down Laurie's cheeks and the lump was re-forming in Leslie's throat.

"Do you want to see him?" Laurie asked. "He looks so precious when he's sleeping."

"No, not right now," Leslie whispered. She didn't dare. Facing her approaching loneliness, she knew the pain would return and she wanted no temptations to pull at her. She could not question her decision until she was far away. She did what was right for little Brooks. Her pain did not matter.

"Hi, my name is Ellen," the woman said.

Kay looked over the top of her magazine and nodded briefly.

"I'm in the room with you," Ellen said.

"I know," Kay replied without looking up again.

She forced herself to concentrate on the article she'd been glancing at. Early in the week Kay had been granted lounge privileges. It hadn't come any too soon, for the day before she'd also been given a roommate. If Kay had been confined to her room for one more day with Ellen she would've become the mental case everyone thought she was.

At first, it had been a real pleasure to be able to stroll the hallways and sit in the lounge. Unfortunately Ellen had the same privileges and had attached herself to Kay, following her around the corridors and sitting with her in the lounge.

"You look nice."

Kay looked up into the woman's vacant eyes. Ellen was about the same size as herself and her figure was about as good as Kay's, but the resemblance ended there. The woman was slovenly about her personal appearance; she didn't take care of her hair or keep herself neat or clean in any way.

"You could look nice too, if you took care of yourself," Kay said.

"I don't want to."

"That's your choice," Kay snapped. "And I really don't care. Now go away and stop pestering me."

Ellen went off to sit in a corner, pouting and glaring at Kay. As long as the woman stopped bugging her, Kay didn't care what she did. Ellen was just one of many annoyances at Willow Haven. She had to get out of this place, Kay thought. She'd been pressing Dr. Bradford about her release date, but he kept putting her off. Maybe it was time to put the screws to the good doctor when he came in today.

"You have a visitor, Mrs. Thurston."

Kay's darkening mood quickly lightened. Derek. His visits were the only ray of sunshine in this high-quality prison. Her hands went automatically to brush and pat at her hair.

"Hello, Kay."

A cloud covered her sunshine as Kay's stomach turned at the saccharine-sweet voice.

"Hello, Suzanne," she grumbled.

Suzanne sat down, putting a box on the table beside her. "This looks like a real nice place. There's all kinds of flowers on the grounds."

"I wouldn't know," Kay snapped. "I haven't progressed to yard privileges yet."

The broad smile stayed in place on Suzanne's face. "So how are you?" she asked.

"I'm fine," Kay said. "Now all I have to do is convince my idiot doctor of that fact."

"Oh, don't push anything, Kay. I mean this is just great. You have a nice room. They serve you your meals. I understand they even have a swimming pool here. It sounds like a resort to me."

"I'm glad you feel that way," Kay said. "I'll tell Dr. Bradford to arrange for a trade today."

Suzanne's laughter pealed through the lounge. "Kay dear, you're such a card." Suddenly Suzanne leaned forward and whispered, "Why is that woman staring at us?"

"That's Ellen," Kay said in a normal voice. "She's one of the guests at this resort. Why don't you go and introduce yourself? Maybe the two of you could have a game of tennis."

Ellen walked over and stood before the two of them.

"What's in the box?" she asked.

They ignored her.

"I want it," Ellen said, reaching for the gift-wrapped box.

Suzanne snatched it to her chest as Kay barked, "Go away."

The woman glared at them both, then shuffled off down the hall. Suzanne returned the box to the table.

"As you can see," Kay said, "the surroundings here at Willow Haven tend to wear on one after a while."

"You can read and watch television here," Suzanne pointed out.

Kay laughed. "I can't take care of my husband's needs here."

Suzanne squealed in laughter and Kay frowned. It was obvious that Suzanne would fit right in with the Willow Haven clientele.

"Oh, Kay," Suzanne said, patting her on the knee. "Don't worry yourself about him. I'm taking care of things while you're gone."

Kay's hands gripped the arms of her chair. "Oh, are you?" she asked. "And just what things are you taking care of?"

"Just ordinary things," Suzanne said, waving her hands gaily.

Kay's stomach tightened. "What do you consider ordinary things?" She forced the words through clenched teeth, feeling her cheeks grow warm.

"Oh, you know. I make sure he eats and has clean clothes for work. You know, that kind of thing."

"We have servants," Kay said. "You needn't bother yourself."

Suzanne shook her head. "You should know Derek by now," she said. "He needs a woman looking after him. I admit that Derek has his good points, but basically he's a little boy. And little boys like a mommy to take care of them."

Kay's hot anger slowly turned into a cold rage. She didn't have all the pieces in place yet, but the overall picture of her problems was coming into focus. And Suzanne was at the center.

Perhaps Kay had underestimated the woman. When they had first met, Kay had decided that Suzanne was just a weakling who would try to worm her way back into Derek's favor by getting him to feel sorry for her. Obviously that hadn't worked, so she had come groveling to Kay. At first, Suzanne had been amusing, but then as time wore on Kay found a certain affection in her heart for the little mouse. And it was nice to have a friend completely dependent on her. Or so she had thought.

"Well, I have to run," Suzanne said, springing up. "Derek needs some new dress shirts, and I'm going shopping with him." She shook her head and laughed. "I tell you, Kay. When we were married the only thing that man could buy without help was a candy bar or an ice cream cone. And he hasn't changed a bit."

Kay stared at her. While Kay was locked up here that woman had free access to her husband. And she certainly was making the best of it. Kay's anger now turned inward. Stupid, so stupid. To trust this woman and to underestimate her. Stupid.

"Oh, I almost forgot. I brought you a present," Suzanne said. "It's from Derek and me. Derek said they're your favorites."

Kay accepted the box without thinking. She was going to get out of this place, today.

"Bye, bye, Kay." Suzanne pecked the air at the side of Kay's cheek. "Take care."

Kay sat there steaming with anger as the sounds of Suzanne's heels echoed down the hallway. Today. No more pussyfooting and playing around. She was getting out of here.

"That's a pretty box."

God! Ellen was the last thing she needed hanging around right now. Kay sprang up. "Go away," she snapped. "And stop bugging me. If you come around me again I'll throw you out the window."

She stormed to the nurses' station. "I want to see Dr. Bradford. And I want to see him now."

"Dr. Bradford is scheduled for rounds this afternoon," the nurse said without looking up from the notes she was making to patients' charts.

With a sweep of her arm, Kay sent the charts flying to the floor. She grabbed the nurse's sleeve, pulling her forward. "Look, you little twit," she hissed. "My money pays your salary and it pays Dr. Bradford. In fact, I have enough money to buy this whole damn place, and I may do it just for the pleasure of burning it down."

"Mrs. Thurston," the nurse said as she tried to control the trembling in her voice. "You are forcing me to call an orderly."

"I'm forcing you to get my doctor, you idiot. Now do it."

"I'll—I'll try."

"I want to speak to him right now," Kay said. "So if he can't come here, have him call me." She turned on her heel and stomped to her room.

Ellen was standing at the door to their room, her eyes wide but still empty.

"Go away, you fool," Kay said through clenched teeth. "Go away."

Kay slammed the door behind her, threw the box on the bed, and herself into a chair. Incompetents and fools. The world was filled with both. She bit her knuckles in fury. Anybody that took her for a fool was a bigger fool. The telephone rang, and Kay snatched it up.

"Yes."

"Kay. Dr. Bradford here. I hear that you've been rather tense this morning."

"I want out."

"In due time, Kay. In due time."

"Don't give me that crap," Kay shouted. "I want out. I'm not sick."

"If you're not sick, then why are you hallucinating?"

Kay clenched her fists and took a deep breath. "I'm not hallucinating anymore. It was probably just some bad food or bad liquor. I'm well now."

"I'm not sure of that," Dr. Bradford said. "I need some more observations and a few more tests."

"You're just screwing around to make more money," Kay said. "I'll pay you double what you'll make on my being in here. Get me out."

"A few more days, Kay. Just a few more days, please."

Kay clenched her teeth. A few more days? What could Suzanne do with Derek and a few more days?

151

"Why don't I give you grounds privileges?" Dr. Bradford suggested. "It would do you good to get out. The grounds are quite nice this time of the year."

That's what Suzanne said. The heat of anger boiled up again and burned her cheeks. Damn it.

"I'll call the nurse. You can go out immediately."

Kay was about to protest, but then clamped her mouth shut. It wasn't what she wanted, but the more she argued, the more he seemed to resist. "That'll be fine, doctor."

"That's a good girl, Kay. Trust me. You'll be out in a matter of days."

She wasn't going to trust anybody but herself and, yes, she *would* be out in a matter of days. She'd make sure of it. She hung up, then went into the bathroom to comb her hair.

She was through believing what anyone told her. Suzanne was out to get Derek back, and if Kay didn't do something soon, Suzanne would win. Kay had never lost a man to anybody, and she wasn't about to start now. Not to that little mouse, no matter how much candy the woman brought her.

Kay stopped, her hands frozen on her towel. The candy. Of course, that had to be it. Why else would Suzanne be spending money on expensive chocolates unless they were a weapon in this battle?

Kay sank against the bathroom wall, her mind working furiously. The question was, what was the best way to handle this discovery?

Chapter Nine

Golden Presents

Ellen leaned up close to the wall, pretending to be washing it. She breathed a sigh of relief as the nurse walked by. Sometimes the nurses talked mean to her. Sometimes they got real mad and they made her go to her room. And when they were real, real mad they would lock her in. They would lock her in and they wouldn't let her out no matter how much she cried.

When the nurse turned a corner, Ellen moved quickly to stand by the door to her and Kay's room. Ellen liked Kay. Kay was strong. Kay never cried. Kay could make the nurses do anything she wanted them to.

She listened at the door. There was no sound; maybe Kay was taking a nap. Should she knock or should she go in? Ellen shook her head. She didn't like questions like that. She didn't like any questions. When Kay was around Ellen didn't have to worry about questions.

Her lip quivered and she sniffled. Kay used to be her friend, but she didn't like Kay anymore. Kay was bad to her. Kay hollered at her. Her nose started to run, and Ellen wiped it on the sleeve of her sweater. Then she quickly looked around. Daddy didn't like it when she did that. If he caught her he would yell at her real loud.

The footsteps of the returning nurse startled Ellen, and she quickly began polishing the handle on the door. Oh wow, that was close. She giggled a little. She was getting real good at fooling the nurses. Kay taught her.

The giggle crumpled into a sniffle when she thought of Kay. Why was Kay so bad to her? They used to be real good friends, the best friends in the whole wide world. She would get Kay her drink of water. And when Kay was in the room with her, Ellen would talk to her. Kay didn't have to say anything. Ellen didn't mind. She would talk all by herself. That's because she and Kay were friends.

But they weren't friends anymore. Kay got a pretty box today and wouldn't share. Friends share. So if Kay didn't share, they wouldn't be friends ever again.

Ellen held her hand up, about to knock, but then she let it slowly fall to her side. She could go in. This was her room, too. She didn't have to knock to go into her own room. Kay wouldn't yell at her for coming into her own room.

But Kay wasn't always nice anymore. Would she tell Ellen to go away? A small smile crossed Ellen's lips. If she didn't make a sound, Kay wouldn't know she was there and wouldn't tell her to go away. She slowly pushed the door open.

She held the door open and waited. No one spoke. No one told her to go away. She stood up straighter and smiled nice. Kay wasn't mad at her anymore.

Ellen let herself in and let the door shut behind her. She had on a big smile for Kay. The smile faded as she blinked and looked around the room. Kay wasn't there. But she'd seen her come in.

From the closed bathroom door came the sound of a shower running. The smile returned. Kay was washing. Kay was always doing that. She washed even when she was clean.

Ellen walked over to the dresser. Kay had such pretty things. There were rings, bracelets, and necklaces. And make-up, too. Daddy wouldn't let her wear makeup.

As she turned away, the gift-wrapped

package, lying on the bed, caught her eye. The pretty box that the lady gave Kay. Ellen didn't like the other lady. She had mean eyes.

Ellen tried to look at the other things in Kay's room. She put on some rings, a bracelet, and a necklace. But the soft blue ribbon called for her attention. Ellen liked colors like blue, pink, and yellow. They were nice. In fact, blue was her favorite color.

She came to the foot of the bed. Ellen told herself that she would just look at the package. There were little figures on the wrapping paper. She picked up the package. There were little bunnies on the paper.

She caressed the paper. She liked bunnies. She had a bunny once. Daddy killed it. He said it smelled. Ellen smelled the paper. Bunnies didn't smell. She'd have to tell Daddy.

Carefully, so as not to tear a single bunny, Ellen removed the paper. Then she lifted the cover. Candy! Chocolate candy. She looked at the bathroom door; the shower was still running. She and Kay were friends. Even friends got grumpy with each other sometimes. Ellen bit into a piece of candy. It was so good.

Putting a second piece in her mouth, she went to the dresser again. She picked up the lipstick. She'd make herself pretty like Kay. Ellen had another piece of candy and then picked up a rouge brush. She was going to look real pretty.

As she worked on herself Ellen began looking real pretty. A soft glow of pinks, greens, and yellows encircled her head. Real pretty music filled the room and three angels came down to sing. The floor rocked back and forth, and around and around. Ellen began dancing. Kay was going to be so surprised when she came out of the shower. She was going to say, Oh my, Ellen, you look so pretty.

Two more angels joined in the song and pretty purple pussycats floated on the walls. When Ellen tried to pet them they would just laugh and run away. Ellen kicked off her shoes, and the grass felt cool on her feet.

One of the angels handed Ellen a book of matches. Ellen smiled prettily and thanked the angel. Ellen liked matches. She lit one and beautiful colors floated around the room. A bottle tipped over on the bed. It smelled bad, like something the nurses called alcohol, but the fire made bigger and prettier colors.

Ellen started sweating. The pussycats were snarling at her. They were being bad and she was getting mad. She swatted at the bad pussycats. She hit one of them and hurt her hand. In the next split second, the room was engulfed in a tremendous multicolored sun and Ellen started crying. She knew Daddy was going to be mad, real mad. She had to hide from him.

Ellen might have been worrying, but few of the other patients were. It was a beautiful day, perfect for a last stroll through the gardens before dinner.

But their last moments of peaceful reflection were shattered as an enormous ball of fire burst through the wall of a second-floor room. Glass and metal window framing were thrown into the rose garden, and confusion reigned. Terrified patients ran crying about the ground, pushing at the gates, screaming of the pursuing ball of fire. The gates remained firm, but the fence was climbable and the woods across the road offered a beckoning refuge.

Derek was tying his tie when the doorbell rang. He frowned at his watch. Suzanne wasn't supposed to come here tonight; he'd promised to pick her up for dinner. But when did that woman ever listen?

"Sir?" It was Hobbs's agitated voice. No doubt he didn't approve of his seeing Suzanne. Not that there was anything to it; they were just friends.

"Come in, Hobbs." Derek slipped into his suit coat.

"Sir, there's someone here to see you."

"Yes, I figured it was her—"

"No, sir."

Derek turned with a frown. Hobbs's agitation was more than annoyance at Suzanne's presence.

"It's someone from the nursing home," the old man said.

"Kay?" Derek cried. "Has something happened to Kay?"

But Hobbs just shook his head as Derek sped past him out of the room and down the stairs. Two solemn-faced men were waiting in the foyer. One was Dr. Bradford; the other Derek recognized as the director of the nursing home.

"What happened?" he said, his stomach sinking into his shoes. She'd had another attack, a worse one this time.

"I'm afraid we have some bad news," Dr. Bradford said. "Is there somewhere we can talk?"

What was keeping them from talking right here? Derek wanted to shout. The servants all knew what was happening anyway. Why prolong his torment? But he led them into the sunroom, where they all sat down.

"Well?" he prompted.

"I'm afraid there was a terrible accident

at the home today," the director said slowly. "A fire and an explosion."

Derek's heart stopped. "And Kay?"

"I'm afraid Mrs. Thurston was killed in it."

It was like a hard blow to the stomach, knocking all wind, all thought from his body. "Killed?" he repeated dumbly, then anger rushed in. "How the hell was she killed?" he cried, jumping to his feet. "What kind of place do you run that patients are killed in accidents like that? Aren't there inspections you have to pass? Rules you have to follow? Damn you, you'll pay dearly for your negligence."

The two other men exchanged glances, then Dr. Bradford got to his feet. He put a hand on Derek's arm and drew him back to his chair.

"The fire was in Kay's room, Derek," he told him. "Either she or her roommate started it. The oxygen outlet was opened and everything in the room was immediately destroyed."

Derek winced at the thought.

"In fact," the doctor went on, "Kay's body was so badly burned that it was identified by her wedding ring."

Her wedding ring! Derek gulped and turned away, fighting back the tears. The ring he'd given her. Memories came flooding in—her outrageous proposal to him, the love that had grown after the ceremony, the gifts she'd showered on him to show her love. Her laughter, her strength, her passion.

"I think I'd like to be left alone," Derek said softly.

The others nodded and got to their feet. "It's a tragedy for all of Genoa City," Dr. Bradford said.

Perhaps. Right now, Derek cared only that he'd lost the woman he loved.

"Hey, George. How's life treating you?" Jonas asked as he approached the bar.

"Not too often, sir," George replied. He kept a solemn expression on his face.

Jonas smiled as he slid onto the stool. Bartenders were the same the world over. Cynical and careful.

"I was here the other night," Jonas said. "I don't know if you remember. I'm Mr. Prentiss's friend." He winked quickly at the man.

A faint smile came to George's face. "Yes, sir, I remember."

"The name's Jonas. I got a little club out in Saunderstown. We got a piano, a chanteuse, and a small electric bill."

"Sounds good," George said. Nodding, he paused a moment. "Always thought about having a little place of my own. Never seemed to work out."

Jonas pulled a business card from his pocket and shoved it across the bar. "Ever want a change of scenery, just drop by and see us."

"I'll keep that in mind." He pocketed the card. "What's your pleasure tonight, Jonas?"

He looked at his watch. Leslie was late. "I don't really have a taste for anything," Jonas said. "Just give me some bar whiskey with a lot of ice."

"We have some rotgut for the tourists," the bartender said. "How about I pour you a couple fingers of Chivas Regal?"

"Sure." Jonas looked at his watch again.

"Hi." It was Leslie, beautiful enough to steal his breath away. "I'm sorry I'm late."

"I got nothing better to do with my life," Jonas said.

Leslie said nothing, just looking down and checking the clasp on her purse.

"You want a table?" he asked.

She nodded.

"Go find a nice dark corner," Jonas ordered. "I'll get you a glass of Chablis."

A moment later, he put a bottle of George's finest Chablis and a glass in front of Leslie, then sat down at the small corner himself. "To us," he said, lifting the glass.

Leslie seemed to fade as she stared at him. Pushing the wineglass away, she said, "That's been a rather popular toast lately."

"I mean it," Jonas replied.

No sooner had the words left his lips than Jonas wanted to retrieve them. They seemed to cause her pain, and that was the last thing he wanted to do.

"I think everybody means what they say, Jonas. At least what they say to me."

They sat in silence, Jonas sipping at his drink and Leslie twirling her glass slowly.

"I told the hotel to keep your room for you," Jonas said.

"Oh, Jonas," Leslie said. "You shouldn't have done that. I told you I had a place of my own in Genoa City."

"Yeah, but you haven't been there for a while. Something could have been broken or you don't have any sheets or something."

"Everything was fine," Leslie said with a small smile. "Besides, the only thing that I really love in the whole world is there."

"Thing?"

The smile stayed small and her eyes were so weary. Jonas wanted to take her in his arms and protect her forever.

"Yes," she said. "Thing. It's not a person, but I love it. And when we are together, it comes to life."

"You got a piano there."

She put her chin in her hands, looking off to a space far in back of his head. "When I sit down at it I enter another world," she said. "It's filled with old friends from all over the world. Beethoven, Liszt, Schubert."

"I heard of 'em," Jonas said, nodding his head. "Myself, I like the stuff you play at the club better, but I always figured that someone with your talent could put an angel's choir to shame."

"You're such a kind man, Jonas."

The softness of her smile covered her eyes, and Jonas felt a sinking sensation in the pit of his stomach. Fear made his breathing come hard. His tongue refused to function.

"I'm going back on tour," Leslie said. "Paris, London, Rome. I'm going back to the only place in this world where I belong."

His heart was pounding. Jonas took a deep breath and exhaled slowly. "Why don't we take your piano and set it up someplace near the club?" he said. "That way I can take care of it. Keep it polished and tuned. Then you and the piano would always have a place to come to. A place to relax and a place where you will always be taken care of."

Leslie shook her head.

"I love you, kid," he said. "I love you more than life itself."

Leslie had to look away from Jonas. The earnest pleading in his face was enough to bring tears to her eyes. She had to leave. She couldn't carry the burden of love anymore. Jonas's love and Lucas's love. It was too much.

"You deserve more than that, Jonas."

"Let me decide what I deserve," he said harshly.

"No, Jonas, no," she implored him. "You should have a woman by your side every day and in your bed every night. You deserve children to keep the goodness of your heart in this world."

"Leslie—"

"No, Jonas." She took his hands in hers. "I love my music. I belong to it. It owns me, body and soul."

Hope burned fiercely in his eyes. "I don't mind coming in second," he said.

"Music is first, second, and more for me. I don't even have room for my—" She paused for a moment and swallowed hard to drive the lump down. "I wouldn't even have room for a child."

"You don't know that."

"I do, dear Jonas. I do."

They stared into each other's eyes. She felt his hands grow cold beneath hers.

Finally, Leslie pulled her hands away and took up her purse.

"I'll never forget you, dear Jonas. You were there in my hour of need. You will always be with me in a special corner of my memory."

She stood up and kissed him on the forehead, and then she was gone.

Jonas stared a long time at the full glass of wine sitting on the table in front of him. The goblet floated in the blur that his eyes formed.

After several minutes his vision cleared and his breathing became less labored. Fate didn't smile on Jonas very often; he'd thought that an exception would be made in Leslie's case. She was the only woman he'd ever really loved. But just when he'd opened his heart to receive her, she was snatched from him. Never to return.

"Well, that's the way the old ball bounces," he muttered to himself. It was time to go home and forget, something he'd done before over the years. But somehow he thought it would be harder this time. He rose and went to the bar.

"Hey, George," he called. "Are you married?"

The bartender shrugged. "A little bit."

"Then get yourself a girl friend for the night and enjoy that bottle of Chablis that you opened. Have a ball on me."

"I can put a temporary cork on it," George said. "You can take it home with you."

"Home." Jonas spat out a short, bitter laugh. "My home is Saunderstown, George. They'd run me out of town if I puked that high-price stuff out into their gutters. We're more into early Thunderbird."

"Hey, Jonas," George called to him.

Jonas stopped and turned.

"You know what my daddy always told me?" George asked. "He said a woman was just like a train. You miss one, don't worry about it. There'll be another along."

Jonas gave George a snappy salute. He wasn't planning on worrying about anything. And he wasn't planning on waiting too long, either. The damp evening air stung his eyes as he stepped outside. He wiped at them with the sleeve of his coat, and they were just fine.

Chapter Ten

Partings

"I can still drive you to O'Hare airport," Lucas offered.

Leslie stared out at the passing scene of fast-food franchises, garages, and old houses interspersed with open fields that lined the road to Genoa City's little airport. Lucas had pushed very hard to drive her to Chicago's international airport. That would have been a three-hour trip —three hours alone with Lucas in the car, and she just wasn't up to that. This way Laurie and Lance and Brooks could come with them. She held her tongue, hoping that Lucas would give up.

"It's all expressway driving," Lucas said. "It would be no problem at all."

"I already have my tickets," Leslie said.

"How long are you going to be in New York?" Laurie asked.

Leslie hoped that their mental telepathy

was operative and she sent her sister a silent, but fervent, thank-you.

"Probably about three days," Leslie said. "I'll get in late tonight and meet with my agent and the tour managers tomorrow. Then the next day I'll have to review my arrangement with my musical director."

"Sounds like a lot of work," Lance said.

"Yes," she replied. "That's why I want to leave Friday. I want to spend Saturday and Sunday in Paris. That's always been my favorite city."

"Do you miss it?"

Leslie didn't turn around. She knew Lance was talking to Laurie.

Laurie responded in a low, satisfied murmur. "Not at all. I have everything I've ever wanted, right here in Genoa City."

Leslie bit her lower lip and turned back to concentrating on the passing scene. She was leaving a big part of herself in Genoa City, but it was for the best. The one thing she'd had trouble reconciling in all this was her love for Lance. She'd turned away two fine men who loved her truly because she loved her sister's husband.

Enough memories had returned to ease her guilt pangs, for she had known Lance before Laurie and their child had been

conceived before his and Laurie's whirl-
wind courtship, but still the ache was
there. The fear that she might never love
again as she loved Lance. Yet she would
do nothing, say nothing. She'd had her
own chance with Lance and had turned
him down. Laurie had him now, him and
their child. It was how it had to be.

"You be careful in New York," Lucas
warned her, breaking her moodiness.

"Lucas." Leslie sighed. "I'm taking a
limousine to the Pierre, then I'll go by cab
to the Lincoln Center offices. Tonight I'll
eat in the hotel and every other day I'll be
eating my meals with two or three other
people."

Silence descended on their car. No, she
wouldn't be alone. There would always be
someone with her. No matter where she
was in the world. But none of those people would be people she loved. She would
never try that again. She just couldn't
carry the responsibility of love. The only
thing she could comfortably love was her
music. It made demands of her, but not
those another person made. She didn't
know why she could handle the demands
of her music and not the emotional demands of a lover, but she didn't care. She
just accepted herself as she was.

Lucas pulled into the airport. "That's

the little thing that's going to take you to Chicago?'' Lucas asked, pointing at the two-engine air taxi sitting on the runway.

Leslie heard the offer in his voice to drive her to Chicago, but she wanted to get away as soon as possible. "It looks light enough to stay up in the air," she said brightly. "It's the big ones that I worry about. I'll never understand how something that weighs tons and tons can float through the air."

"Magic," Lance answered, laughing. No one joined him.

"I'll get your bags," Lucas said.

Leslie just nodded and got out to stand looking across the fields beyond the airstrip. Behind her she could hear Lance helping Laurie and Brooks out of the car, but she didn't look that way, pretending instead that her thoughts, her dreams, were all fastened to that little plane awaiting her. When she heard the trunk lid slam, Leslie started moving slowly toward the entryway. As she expected, Lucas caught up with her and walked by her side, Lance and Laurie following behind.

Leslie went to the ticket counter and Lucas put her bags on the scale as she surrendered her tickets to the agent.

"Check your bags straight through to New York's Kennedy Airport, ma'am?"

"Yes," Leslie said. "Except for the small

white one." She looked among the pile of bags. "I want to carry that on."

"I figured you would." It was Lance speaking. "I have it."

How did he know that she'd want to carry her music with her? Did they still have that magical communication that lovers have? "Oh, good," Leslie replied. She did not turn around. She couldn't think about that now. "Thank you."

"Air Wisconsin, flight one-two-eight," the agent said, handing Leslie her ticket packet. "You'll be leaving in twenty minutes from gate B."

"Can I get on now?" Leslie asked.

"In a few minutes."

"Well, I might as well get going," Leslie said to Lucas.

"We'll walk with you," he said.

With a sense of relief, Leslie noticed from the corner of her eye that Lucas had taken her carry-on bag from Lance. She didn't need to feel that bond anymore. She led the way to gate B, then turned, holding out her hand to Lucas.

"It looks like they're letting us board," she said.

He looked at his watch. "You have almost eighteen minutes before departure."

"I know," Leslie said, almost pulling her bag off his shoulders. "But I like to get a seat by the window and generally settle myself down. I don't like to rush onto a plane like it was a bus."

Couldn't he sense how painful this was? What good could another eighteen do? She was leaving her heart and her child behind. She didn't need another eighteen minutes of saying good-bye.

Lucas nodded his head and let her put the bag on her shoulder. He looked at her face, then at the ground. Leslie could see tiny muscles twitch and pull in his face. She gave him a quick hug and an even quicker kiss. Prolonging the pain would be cruel to him, too.

"Good-bye, Leslie." His voice was husky, his eyes misty. "I'll be here waiting as long as the Lord above allows me. My heart is yours and you can come take it whenever you want."

She wanted to cry and hug him to her breast. Not as a lover, but because she felt so sorry for the poor man. He'd lived in Lance's shadow all his life and now he couldn't even have the woman he loved.

"Lucas," she whispered. "My heart belongs to my music. I've tried giving it to a man, but then the music snatches it back."

"I could change that if you let me try," Lucas said.

Leslie just shook her head. They'd tried that before, when he'd married her, knowing she was pregnant with Lance's child, yet certain he could win her love. She had been desperate to let him try, but he hadn't succeeded then, and there was no way he could convince her to let him try again. They'd both suffered too much from her weakness in agreeing last time. She pulled away from Lucas and Lance came around to hug her. Leslie steeled herself. Make it quick, make it quick.

He kissed her on the cheek, then she pulled back. "Good-bye, Lance," she said, quietly but briskly. "Take care of Laurie." There was nothing else to say to him. Nothing else she could say.

She turned again and looked out the window of the plane. There were some baby sounds behind her as Brooks was transferred from Laurie's arms to Lance's.

Laurie put a hand on Leslie's arm and suddenly they were hugging each other. They held each other tight in a duet of quiet sobs. Neither could say a word and Leslie finally pushed herself away. She picked up her bag and rushed for the plane.

At the top of the stairs she stopped, turning for one last look. Lance and Lucas blurred as Laurie, with Brooks in her arms, came into focus. A sharp pain ripped at Leslie's heart and a cry burst past her lips.

"Are you all right, ma'am?" the cabin attendant asked.

Leslie nodded and hurriedly brushed by her to take a seat alone in back. She clenched her teeth so hard that they hurt. Leslie ground them, but the pain nowhere matched that in her heart. She almost prayed for the amnesia to return.

COMMUNITY LEADER DIES IN FIRE.

Jill looked at the headlines screaming at her from the front page of the Genoa City newspaper, Stuart Brooks's publication.

The story went on to say that Mrs. Kay Chancellor Thurston had been recovering at the Willow Haven Sanitarium from a severe case of exhaustion. Jill snickered. Rumors were flying about town that dear Kay had turned into a hophead. She had taken so many drugs that the doctor had committed her to Willow Haven so that he could figure out her contents.

But then Jill winced as she read the paragraphs about Kay's being burned beyond recognition. Even though Jill hated Kay, she had to admit it was a horrible way to die.

The rest of the article outlined Kay's various businesses and the different charitable boards that she served on. Surviving was husband Derek.

Jill threw the paper on the floor, her

heart racing with excitement. Derek was free and available. Not only that, but he was a new and improved Derek. She'd seen that Kay had smoothed many of his rough edges and whatever ones she missed would be covered by Kay's money.

Jill sprang up, dancing around the room. She screamed, releasing the pent-up excitement and energy that grew in her. She was certainly sorry that Kay died, especially the way she did, but that was no fault of hers. And now that Kay was gone, Jill had no intention of letting the grass grow under her feet. Derek was there for the plucking.

A slight frown crossed Jill's face. His ex-wife, a Suzanne something or other, was in town. Jill had heard that she was a mousy sort, but it was still best to move fast.

She called and told Stuart's secretary that she would be there to see him within thirty minutes, then she flew into her bedroom to shower and dress. Derek was free. A significantly enhanced Derek. Jill laughed and laughed in the sheer joy of it, calming herself slightly as she entered Stuart's reception area.

"Would you like to sit down, Mrs. Brooks?" the gray-haired woman coolly asked. "Mr. Brooks is on the phone right now. He'll be off soon."

"He can get off now," Jill snapped, and marched into Stuart's office, ignoring the woman's protests.

Stuart's initial reaction was to drop his jaw to his chest. He recovered quickly, his look of wonderment supplanted with a dark frown. "I'm sorry," he said into the telephone. "An emergency has come up. I'll have to call you back."

"Mr. Brooks, I'm sorry. I told her you were on the telephone, but she just—"

"That's quite all right, Mrs. James. I know it's not your fault," he said. "Please close the door behind you."

"Yes, sir," Mrs. James replied dutifully, and left.

Jill swept over to a chair and sat down, crossing one leg over the other. "Does that woman have any children?" Jill asked with a smirk.

"Why?" Stuart still wore his mask of dark anger.

"The way she hovers and protects you, one would think that there are some frustrated mother instincts at work." Then an evil grin took control of Jill's face and filled it with maliciousness. "Or maybe the poor old thing has the hots for her boss."

The red flag of rage climbed Stuart's neck and into his face. "Mrs. James is—" Then he clenched his jaw shut for a moment. "What do you want?"

"Be nice to me, Stuart. I've come bearing gifts."

"What evil game are you playing now?"

Jill stared at him for a long moment. In some ways she was going to miss Stuart. Old gentlemen like him could be so amusing. No matter how angry you got them, they still felt constrained to treat you like some delicate flower. But Derek would give her much more of what she needed.

"I'm going to give you your freedom," Jill said.

Confusion and disbelief flashed through Stuart's eyes like the strobe lights in a discotheque. Jill watched in amusement as he stewed. It wasn't often that one got such delicious revenge. The bastard hadn't even looked at her since that night in Las Vegas. He certainly wouldn't have been her first choice as a lover, but she did have her needs and he hadn't done anything to meet them.

"Why?" he asked. Suspicion brought order to Stuart's emotions.

"Because I want to."

"How much is it going to cost me?" he asked.

Jill was about to reply, "Nothing," but she paused. Derek wasn't going to jump into her bed right away. She would be needing a little pin money until she got things in order.

"Just a little spending money, Stuart. That's all."

"How little?"

She had to laugh at the poor man. "Relax, Stuart. I'm not going to burn you. I don't need you anymore."

"How much?"

"Five thousand a month for a year."

He stared at her in silence.

Jill could feel her stomach tighten. "Well?"

"Well, what else?" he asked.

Relief caused her to laugh out loud. "That's it, Stuart. Nothing else."

He turned his back to her and stared out the window. Stuart sat there and stared for a long, long time. Jill was sure that he would accept her offer, but she didn't want to upset anything.

Finally, he said, "See my lawyer. He'll take care of all the details."

"Good," she said. She stood to leave, but something held her back. He really hadn't been too bad a guy. Sure he had ignored her, but she had pulled a dirty trick on him.

He must have known she was still there, but he refused to turn around. "When will you be gone?" he asked.

"Well," she said with some hesitation. "I still have my old place. I guess I could be out by late this afternoon."

"Thank you." He seemed carved from stone, his voice a still rumble.

"There's no need to rise, Stuart. I can see myself out."

He didn't reply and Jill quickly left. Mrs. James didn't even look up as Jill swished by. Boy, it was good to be rid of Stuart and his old crowd, Jill thought. She was young and needed to be among young people. People with an appreciation for life and the capability to enjoy it.

Stuart sat at his chair, staring out the window. His throat hurt from the enormous lump that was crowding within it. He didn't know whether to laugh or cry.

Slowly the lump dissolved somewhat, and when he could trust himself to speak, Stuart pressed his intercom button.

"Yes, Mr. Brooks."

He took a deep breath and let it out slowly. Then he spoke in a husky voice, barely above a whisper. "Mrs. James, would you please do me a great favor? Call Mrs. Foster and see if she's able to receive a guest within the hour."

Liz's house wasn't that far from his office, but Stuart spent most of the hour just driving around. He needed that much time to settle his nerves.

At first he could not believe his good fortune. He knew that Jill had to have an ulterior motive. She certainly wasn't giving him his freedom out of the goodness of her heart. Then things began to fall into place. Jill had pulled her stunt soon after Derek Thurston had married Kay Chancellor. Now Kay Chancellor was dead. Burned to a crisp in that awful explosion and fire at the Willow Haven Sanitarium. He remembered enough of his basic science to know that fire required oxygen to burn. Apparently oxygen had leaked into Kay's room. That would be enough to produce a momentary ball of fire powerful enough to melt a steel blast furnace.

That tragedy had freed Derek, which in turn freed himself. Stuart felt a momentary sense of guilt at his joy, but he had nothing to do with Kay's misfortune. The world turned like a roulette wheel; there were winners and losers. Even the sobering thought that this condition was temporary and that all of them were nothing but playing chips for the gods failed to dampen his mood. He pointed his car to Liz Foster's home.

Liz greeted him very tentatively. "Hello, Stuart," she said quietly as she stood back to let him enter.

Stuart took off his coat and walked right into her living room, but rather than sit across from her, he went to her window and looked out. For a moment he feared that he would break down, right before the woman he loved, but the gods listened to his prayers and gave him the necessary control for his emotions. He turned to face her.

"Liz," he said. "I'm free."

There was silence, then in that gentle and quiet voice she showed why he loved her so. Her thoughts were always for others, for the helpless. "What about the child?" she asked.

"There is no child, Liz. She was never pregnant."

"Never?"

"She admitted the whole thing. She'd faked the letter on some stationery she stole from the doctor's office. I should have called to verify it, but I never did. She gambled on that and won."

She could have gotten pregnant. He had made love to her. Stuart was sure that that thought was also in Liz's mind. At first, he was thankful for her silence, but then, as it dragged out, that silence became a cold and heavy burden. He turned back to the window, but finally could stand the silence no longer.

"Liz, my dearest. Can you ever forgive an old fool?"

Muffled sobbing caused him to spin around. He rushed to her. "Liz, please, please," he murmured in her hair. "I'm so sorry. Please don't cry."

She lifted up her face to his and, though tear-stained, it had a certain glow. "I cry when I'm happy, my love. When I'm so happy my heart is about to burst."

They clutched at each other. The world turned away while their tears flowed, washing away the stains of sin and the pain of despair.

After a while the world came back and brought with it blue skies and sunshine. Stuart gave Liz his handkerchief. "You know, Stuart," she said between ladylike sniffs. "There's a justice of the peace over in—"

"No," he said firmly. Then, seeing the concern in her eyes, he clutched her in his arms. "You don't deserve anything so cheap. My lawyer will clear things up in a few days, and then I thought we could go see the Reverend Brown. A small wedding in the parsonage would be nice."

The joy in her eyes erased all the pain Stuart's life had ever known. "Whatever you say," she murmured into his chest.

Chapter Eleven

Out of the Ashes

The long line of cars snaked behind the limousine, creeping along the narrow cemetery drive. The limo stopped behind the hearse and Derek climbed stiffly out. Suzanne and Jill were both with him and he was glad. These last few days had been unbearable. He hadn't realized how much he loved Kay until she was gone. They waited as the pallbearers took the casket from the hearse and carried it slowly up the hill to the gravesite.

"She was a fine woman," Jill said to him, squeezing his arm and giving him an admiring smile.

Derek nodded. He knew that Jill and Kay hadn't gotten along, but he was touched to see how Jill shared his grief.

Singly and in couples, the mourners filed up from their cars to gather in a mass around Kay's grave. All their friends were there, Derek realized with gratitude. Kay had been well liked and well respected, a leader in Genoa City. He took a deep breath, willing the pain to subside, though he knew it wouldn't. Not yet. Would there ever come a time when it would fade?

"My friends," the minister began. "It is truly a sad day for us all."

Derek closed his eyes, the wind ruffling his hair as he listened to the minister's somber intonations.

Far down the drive, a taxi cab slowed and stopped at the gates to the cemetery. "Drop me here," its passenger ordered, then slipped the driver a ten-dollar bill. "And wait. I'll be back after the funeral."

The driver turned in his seat, looking back at the heavily veiled woman. "You know the old lady?" he asked curiously.

There was a definite chill in the air. "You mean Mrs. Thurston?"

"Yeah. You know her?"

"In a way," the woman said. She withdrew from the cab. The wind tugged at her veil, but she held it securely in place as she walked through the gates.

Carefully, unobtrusively, she walked over the grassy expanses until she reached the edges of the crowd. From where she stood she could see Derek and Suzanne and Jill, but it was to Suzanne that her gaze kept returning. Suzanne, the ex-wife. Suzanne, the friend. Suzanne, the murderer.

Under the cover of her veil, Kay Chancellor Thurston smiled. Revenge had always been one of her favorite sports.

COLUMBIA PICTURES
presents
YOUNG AND RESTLESS
Official Licensed Merchandise

For **FREE** brochure of all
merchandise, send a self addressed,
stamped, LEGAL size envelope to:

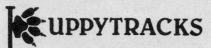**UPPYTRACKS**

**6513 Lankershim Blvd.
No. Hollywood, California 91606**